★ BROADWAY BABY ★

ALSO BY ALAN SHAPIRO

PROSE

The Last Happy Occasion

Vigil

In Praise of the Impure

POETRY

The Courtesy

After the Digging

Happy Hour

Covenant

Mixed Company

The Dead Alive and Busy

Song & Dance

Tantalus in Love

Old War

Night of the Republic

TRANSLATION

The Oresteia by Aeschylus

The Trojan Women by Euripides

BROADWAY BABY

a novel by

ALAN SHAPIRO

Algonquin Books of Chapel Hill 2012

Published by
ALGONQUIN BOOKS OF CHAPEL HILL
Post Office Box 2225
Chapel Hill, North Carolina 27515-2225

a division of
WORKMAN PUBLISHING
225 Varick Street
New York, New York 10014

Printed in the United States of America.
Published simultaneously in Canada by Thomas Allen & Son Limited.
Design by Anne Winslow.

LIBRARY OF CONGRESS CATALOGING-IN-PUBLICATION DATA
Shapiro, Alan, [date]
Broadway baby : a novel / by Alan Shapiro.—1st ed.
p. cm.
ISBN 978-1-56512-983-2
1. Ambition—Fiction. 2. Actresses—Fiction. 3. Motherhood—Fiction.
4. Families—Massachusetts—Boston—Fiction. I. Title.
PS3569.H338B76 2011
813'.54—dc22 2011020656

10 9 8 7 6 5 4 3 2 1
First Edition

★ FOR E.F. THE ONE AND ONLY

★ BROADWAY BABY ★

OVERTURE

Clutching her playbill she followed the usher through the golden doors and down the carpeted center aisle. She looked at the big stage, the gold-tasseled burgundy folds of the massive curtains, the gigantic tableau of dead stars in postures of woe or ecstasy on the ceiling; she felt enveloped by the excited murmur of the audience all around her, the lazy chaotic sounds of the musicians tuning up. The usher led her toward the stage past row after row of the most elegant people, all radiant as celebrities, maybe some of them were celebrities, who knows?—they all could see her being led to even better seats than theirs, the seats her son had reserved for her. The stage grew larger with every step; she could see the heads of the musicians in the pit, the wrinkles in the back of the conductor's tux. Their seats were three rows from the stage, dead center, right in front of Mayor Guiliani!

Her younger son said, “Ma, stop looking around, aren’t these seats good enough for you?”

“Miriam,” her husband said, “you’ll bust a blood vessel if you don’t relax. You’re embarrassing us. Just look at the playbill.”

But she was too excited to look at the playbill; besides, she wanted to maximize the surprise!

After all those years of training, her dragging him kicking and screaming to dance lessons and voice lessons, all the struggle and disappointment he had endured when he was starting out, and that she herself had endured for his sake, here he was at last, her son, on Broadway, just as she had always dreamed. Maybe now he’d thank her. And if he didn’t, so what? His having gotten here, his happiness, was thanks enough.

The lights dimmed. When the orchestra struck the first note, and the audience applauded, she was leaning forward; even as it started, she wanted the overture over with already, she wanted the curtains to part and her son (whichever character he was) to appear. She could hardly breathe; it was as if her heart were beating somewhere outside herself and she couldn’t get it back. At first, she thought maybe she was too excited and that’s why she didn’t spot him right away when the curtain finally opened on the bright stage and the actors playing actors hurried every which way before her (“gotta run, gotta run, let’s have lunch”). He wasn’t Joe, he wasn’t Artie, or de Mille, or Sheldrake, not even the least of the lesser characters (“I’m shooting a Western down at Fox” “How can you work with Daryl?” “We should talk”). Where was he? She couldn’t spot him, not even when the whole ensemble divided into different groups, and each one in turn was singing "gotta run," "gotta run," "let's have lunch," "gotta run." Had she missed him? She turned to her husband and said, "Did you see him?"

"What?" he said.

"Did you see him?" She was almost hyperventilating.

Her younger son put his hand on her arm and squeezed it. "Ma," he said, "take it easy; he's one of the cops, he's there, right there, to the right of the star, a little behind him."

People were turning around and scowling. She heard someone behind her, was it the mayor? say, "Lady, keep it down, will you?"

"One of the cops?" she said.

"One of the cops, yes, right there."

She said, "There must be some mistake!"

"Lady," the voice behind her hissed, "If you don't shut up, I'll call the usher!"

Center stage, Joe Gillis ended the first number with, "Come to get your knife back? It's still there, right between my shoulder blades."

One of the cops, one of the nameless cops! Was he even mentioned in the playbill? But she had twisted the playbill into a crooked stalk and her hands were shaking too much to untwist it.

"Is that it?" she said out loud to no one.

"Ma," her youngest said, "Jeez, will you just stop?"

"There he is again," her husband said. And he pointed, but

by the time she looked the stage had gone dark, and then the second number started, "Every Movie's a Circus."

Now she was trying to thumb through the playbill, to smooth out the pages, looking for her son's name in the darkness and so again she didn't see him when he came on stage in the role of an actor telling another actor about a role he's landed in a new blockbuster picture; he said, "I'm a policeman. 'Hang up punk!' That's all I say." And that's all he said. He didn't appear again in any other scene.

She looked up when her husband nudged her.

"What?" she said.

"Your son," he said.

"My son? He's here somewhere; just give me a minute." And she looked back down at the playbill on her lap; she was carefully stretching it out with her fingers, smoothing it out, searching for her son's name. It was somewhere in the playbill. It had to be.

ACT

Scene I

"Tomorrow I'll be ten years old," Miriam Bluestein told herself as she sat in the bathtub. Ten years old, and in a few days her mother would be taking her to New York City for the first time. She looked out the bathroom window at the bright-lit billboard on the rooftop of Fleischman's Bakery, where all the way from Broadway and the Ziegfeld *Follies,* Fanny Brice looked in at her, at Miriam, here in Mattapan, the singer's shining arms held out, her face smiling, as if to welcome the little girl, now that she wasn't so little anymore, into the company of stars. How many nights during bathtime had she stared at the great singer, the great Jewish performer her grandparents especially, but everybody really, up and down the street and throughout the neighborhood, revered and talked about. How many evenings before bedtime did they listen on the radio to the *Follies* coming to them "from the Ziegfeld Theater in downtown Manhattan," and every time Miss Brice would sing "My Man," or "Second Hand Rose," she and Bubbie would sing along, and afterward Zaydie would look at Miriam and smile a smile that she was sure was saying, imagine the joy she gives her parents. What a blessing such a child would be.

Miriam looked out at Fanny looking in at her, and thought, who knows, maybe in a few days she'd be watching Fanny Brice herself. Maybe someday that would be Miriam up there on a billboard looking in on some other little girl who in a few days would be ten years old and coming to New York City for the first time. Mattapan, Manhattan, they were practically the same word. Only two letters made the difference. Only two letters turned the every day into the never before, the just here into the far away. How had she never noticed that before? Maybe this was what it meant to be ten, almost a teenager, almost an adult. What other new things would she soon be noticing?

Next week she'd be someone who had been to New York City, who'd been to Broadway. No one she knew, not one single person beside her mother, not any of her friends, could say that. Not Zaydie and Bubbie, and certainly not her father, no, not him.

Mattapan, Manhattan. She wrung the sponge out over her head and laughed as the water cascaded down over her face. It wasn't too long ago that Bubbie used to bathe her. Bubbie would lather her up until she wore an ermine stole of suds along her arms and shoulders, and a white tiara on her head, and she would call her "a regular little star, a little Fanny Brice, a Sophie Tucker." Now, of course, she bathed herself the way grown-ups did. It was a funny thing to think about, to try to remember, the last time Bubbie bathed her. There had to have been a last time, though she couldn't recall it, a time like any other time that she and maybe Bubbie, too, believed would just go on forever, and it did, or seemed to, until it didn't, and now she couldn't even find the memory of it. That must have meant there'd come a last time, too, to play with all her dolls and who knew what else. Now that she was older, how many things every day would she be doing for the last time without knowing it, things she would not recall until too late when whatever it was was beyond recalling? Mattapan, Manhattan, Manhattan, Mattapan. She dunked her head under the water and opened her eyes. The blurry shapes of the drain with the white plug in it, her hands, her arms, all of her on the eve of her tenth birthday, a few days before her trip to New York City, were wavering with water shadows, shadows that the bathroom walls and ceiling would later seem to swallow as the water twisted down the drain.

THE NEXT DAY, she was walking home from school down the alley that ran behind her block of buildings when an orange kitten ran out from under a parked car.

Overhead laundry flapped from clotheslines on the back porches in the cold November air. She could hear a baby crying and someone shooing something off a porch. She imagined someone in one of the windows looking out at her, seeing what they thought was just a little girl walking home from school, not realizing what today was or where she'd be come Friday, or who she'd see.

She followed the kitten to some nearby trash bins. It must be hungry; it must be looking for food. "Here kitty, kitty," she called, kneeling on the gravel. She tried to make herself sound younger than she was, the way adults did when talking to little babies, like Fanny Brice as Baby Snooks. But the kitten dashed out and slipped under a neighbor's roadster and out the other side and leaped onto the far corner of a fence, behind some scraggly bushes. She could see it among the leaves, its paws drawn under it, its tail pulled round like a moat. She said, "I won't hurt you, kitty. It's my birthday today; you'll be safe with me." Up and down the alley, dogs were barking; she could hear old Mrs. Leavitt, their next-door neighbor, yelling at her twenty-year-old nephew Joey who'd come to live with her after his parents died of influenza so many years ago. "Maria, Joey? Maria? She's not for you. Maria?" The tabby meowed and kept meowing but it wouldn't budge, and after a while Miriam gave up and went home.

"Bubbie," she asked her grandmother. "Bubbie, there's a lost kitten out back; since it's my birthday, can I keep it?"

"No alley cats," Bubbie said. "I don't care what day it is. The filth, the stink—I don't have enough to do already? Call your big-shot mother at the store, maybe for the rats she'll want it."

"Tula's," her mother said, in the cheerful voice she used at work, only with customers.

"Ma," Miriam said, "there's a kitty out back and, um, well, it's my birthday and . . ."

"Miriam," her mother said, "how many times have I told you

not to call me at the store, I have a business to run, and what does your birthday have to do with anything?"

"Well," she said, "Bubbie says we can't keep a cat here but I was thinking maybe at the store I could keep it; it might help with the mice."

Her mother said, "If you want a cat, just ask for a cat. Don't give me a song and dance about your birthday."

"So, can I have a cat?"

"No."

She decided to keep it anyway. It would be her secret pet. She left a bowl of milk out, near the fence, tucked under the bushes, and an hour later the bowl was empty. But the kitten was still there, still crying, so she brought out a bowl of little bits of tuna and crackers. The kitten still would not approach. It cried as she knelt there, calling to it, and then after a while it simply watched her. But it never consented to be touched, to be petted, which was all that Miriam longed to do. Miriam told herself that eventually the cat would learn how kind she was, how mistaken it was to fear her. She was ten years old. Then she shook the bowl to show the kitten that it was full and not a trap; she shook the bowl, calling out sweet names. But the kitten wouldn't budge, and when she edged a little closer, it just retreated farther back into the bushes, its green eyes glaring at the little girl calling kitty, kitty, come here kitty, holding the bowl out and shaking it, shaking the bowl as if asking for alms.

Scene II

In the predawn dark, the train pulled out of South Station. Miriam had been looking forward to this trip all week, but now that it had started she began to wonder why her mother wanted her along. Sitting across from her, she watched her mother's reflection in the window: in one hand, as always, a cigarette burned at the end of a long white holder while her other hand now and then turned the pages of the big account book in her lap. Thin threads of smoke swirled up from the tip of the cigarette and seemed to wave mournfully at the ghost threads in the window waving back at them. Miriam stared at her mother's bent head floating on the darkness, the yellow curls meticulously tight and flat against her high forehead, the diamond-studded reading glasses perched on the tip of her long nose, and the sealed look of her thin lips, the no-nonsense don't-be-a-bother-to-me look that Miriam knew by heart. She was the most beautiful and best-dressed woman Miriam had ever seen, even more beautiful there, reflected in the window where Miriam could watch her without her mother knowing. She looked like a starlet, though she had no interest in the stage, no interest in music or acting or anything, so far as Miriam could tell, but the store, and her customers, and the business trips to New York City she made so often. Whatever she did when she wasn't working, Miriam had no idea. Her mother was a mystery, a little scary sometimes, but also because of this a little glamorous. But it drove Bubbie and Zaydie crazy how often she was gone, how unavailable she was, how little she had to do with any of them, with Miriam especially.

As the day brightened, she watched her mother's image float there, fainter and fainter while the world passed through it: warehouses, water towers with little ladders running up the sides, a stockyard, some sort of soot-darkened factory or foundry with a giant smokestack gushing the whitest steam she'd ever seen, and then the back of apartment buildings just like the one she lived in with her grandparents.

"Do you think we'll go to the *Follies* and see Fanny Brice, Ma?"

Her mother grunted. Miriam couldn't tell if that meant yes or no.

Later, she was looking through her mother's fading image at back porches strung with laundry, and families in the windows getting ready to go out, mothers and fathers and children, too, half-dressed, eating breakfast, moving from room to room. She had no memory of ever having lived with her mother, much less of her parents ever having lived together like a normal family. Try as she might, she couldn't imagine it. And yet no one, not Zaydie or Bubbie, or her older cousins would ever speak about these things. Whenever she'd ask why her parents had gotten divorced, they'd shrug and change the subject. A family friend once had responded, "Why do cats hate fish and love water?"

Miriam had no idea how her mother, Tula Gore, owner of Tula's, the most fashionable woman's clothing store in Boston, could have fallen in love with Maury Bluestein, a butcher, a "peasant" butcher, a greenhorn, a schmo—wasn't that what her mother called him?

Even Miriam was embarrassed by him on the rare occasions when he would show up at the apartment: shy, awkward, fretful, the opposite of everything her mother was. He'd stand there in the doorway, hemming and hawing, then put a box of something wrapped up in butcher paper in her hand. "For you," he'd mumble. "Use it in good health." No, no, he couldn't come in, no, he wasn't thirsty; he'd just have eaten, or he wouldn't be feeling well and didn't want to make her sick; maybe next time, maybe next time they'd go to lunch or to a picture. She knew her mother's family didn't like him. And she hated herself for feeling funny in his presence, uncomfortable, as if he stood for something bad in her. She'd stare at the stubby fingers of his clumsy hands, the butcher paper, the demoralized tie and jacket. He smelled like meat. She hated herself for the relief she felt when he was gone. It was easier to love him when the love was all anticipated or remembered, disentangled from the awkwardness of standing there together, looked at by the others, judged.

Once, before she knew any better, Miriam asked her mother why she and Papa didn't live together. And Tula stared at Miriam for a long second before saying, "Do I look like a butcher's wife?" No, she didn't, but if you asked Miriam, she didn't look or act much like a mother, either. None of Miriam's friends had parents like hers—a father who visited maybe once a month and a mother who traveled so much on business that she didn't live with her own daughter, never had, though Bubbie brought Miriam to the store each and every Saturday to be with her for a few hours, whether she wanted her there or not.

As THE HOUSES with bigger and bigger yards slid by, Miriam thought about the store and the great nothing to do of her days there, learning to stay out of her mother's way. She pictured the big gold letters of her mother's name emblazoned on the giant window, and beyond the letters the women mannequins in their various poses: one with her hand on her hip, another with a cigarette holder raised halfway to her lips, all of them in wigs of different styles and colors, and all wearing the most marvelous dresses, as if they were royalty at a ball or wedding—halter gowns of crepe-de-chines, or satin, or the new satin look-alike her mother called rayon. The dresses shimmered dreamily behind the golden letters of her mother's name.

She wondered again why her mother wanted to take her on this "buying" trip, since she never had before, no matter how much Miriam had asked or begged—New York was Broadway, and the *Follies,* Fanny Brice and Al Jolson! But until last week, her mother had always said it was no place for a little girl, and anyway she had a business to run and didn't have time to play when she was working. Someday Miriam would thank her for how hard she worked.

She studied her mother's spectral features in the glass as if something in the tilt of her head, or the way the cigarette holder seemed to rise to her lips mechanically on strings of smoke, might somehow disclose the reason why her mother wanted her, this time, to come along.

The train whistle blew and suddenly it seemed the sun rose high enough to blot out all traces of her mother in the window. As if the girl herself had caused the sun to shine too brightly, Tula glanced at Miriam, and then pulled down the shade, and in the semidark continued working. If they had been at the store now, Miriam would have hidden herself within the circular rack of the most expensive skirts and dresses, behind the big pleats and godets, the flaring drapery, the way she always did, so as not to be noticed spying on all the customers who came and went all day. She loved watching them fingering the fabric, taking this or that gown off the rack and holding it up against themselves before the triple panels of the full-length mirror beside the dressing room. It amazed her how those women would enter the dressing room stoop-shouldered or stumpy, lanky or fat, in clothes as humdrum as the women themselves, and emerge a few moments later utterly transformed—their shoulders square, their figures sharpened by the crosscutting of the fabric or hidden by the glittering lamé.

When she was hidden away, unnoticed, Miriam could love her mother best, her store voice, so knowing and confident, telling her customers about the dresses and who designed them and how elegant they made the women look, how perfect their "bosoms" seemed in such a style. There was never any trace of the impatience and annoyance Miriam was used to. In her store, her mother sounded like a trusted friend, a confidante, someone who cared for nothing but the happiness of others. Tula would joke, too, about the absent men, the husbands, jokes that made the men seem like fools, like idiots, though how or why Miriam couldn't quite say. "Oh darling," her mother would exclaim, looking over her customer's shoulder as the woman posed before the mirror, "don't worry about the price! He'll take out a second mortgage just to see you take this off."

Now the train entered a tunnel and slowed to a stop. Her mother pulled up the shade and there she was again in the window, staring in and smiling. It was the same smile Miriam had seen at the store last Saturday. She had been on the phone with someone, and while she talked Miriam drifted to the back room where the mannequins were stored—everywhere there were naked bodies with bald heads, some lying on the floor, some leaning against the walls, others standing together like grown-ups at a party, except without wigs and clothes on they were indistinguishable. She touched one of them on the arm, ran her hand lightly over the swelling of the breast; it was smooth and cold and she didn't understand what all the fuss was about, why the ladies who came to the store cared so much about their "bosoms," and how the gowns and dresses showed them off or failed to. What was the big deal?

On that Saturday, from the back room, she could hear her mother talking—not as she usually did on the phone with businesspeople, saying she wasn't going to "take a fucking," and she would "cut his balls off if he tried to fuck her, did he understand that?" No, this time her voice was soft and low, and though Miriam couldn't quite make out what the words were, it was pleasant to listen to them.

She concentrated so hard, Miriam still had one hand on a mannequin's breast when she looked up to see her mother watching her. Her mother was smiling, her eyebrows raised. There was something in the look that made her blush with shame.

"So, darling," her mother had said then, "how about you come with me next week to New York City, just us girls, isn't that what you've always wanted? We can paint the town and, while we're at it, get your grandmother off my back—what do you say?"

It turned out that the tunnel wasn't just a tunnel; it was a station, too. And now a man entered the car and sat down next to her mother. He was tall and slender; he wore a shiny gray suit, gray fedora tilted back on his head. "Hi'ya doll face," he said. "What do you hear, what do you say?" His name was Mr. Perez. The ring on his left hand glittered; it was like the one Zaydie wore, only bigger and brighter. When he smiled, his left eye seemed to close in a kind of slow wink. He gave Miriam a peppermint and called her Senorita, as if Senorita were her name. For the next few hours, they laughed a lot, Tula and Mr. Perez. Her mother kept touching his arm and laughing. She'd never seemed so warm, so much like a girl. When the train finally arrived at Grand Central Station, the man helped them with their bags to the taxi, then rode with them to the hotel, he and her mother in the backseat, Miriam up front with the driver.

"You stay here, Miriam, understand?" her mother said, seating her daughter under a massive chandelier in the giant hotel lobby. Miriam watched her mother and Mr. Perez disappear into a golden elevator. People hurried through the lobby every which way, some trailed by Negro porters pulling carts piled high with luggage—couples arm in arm, and men in dark suits and hats, swinging briefcases as they strode past, newspapers tucked under an arm. This was not the New York she had imagined; this was a New York full of Tulas and the men she talked with on the phone. If only Bubbie were here, they would have been sitting in the Ziegfeld theater watching Fanny Brice by now. Maybe they would have gone backstage to meet the stars themselves. And afterward, they would have walked hand in hand down Broadway, singing "My Man" or "My Mammy."

Miriam must have dozed off, for when her mother and Mr. Perez returned, she wasn't sure if she was still dreaming. They seemed so happy, the two of them, happy and calm, and it embarrassed Miriam the way her mother held the man's arm and how all through lunch in the hotel restaurant he would look at her mother and smile or kiss her on the neck. They seemed to hardly know that Miriam was there; she could stare at them all she wanted.

Finally Mr. Perez said he had to go—"to see a man about a dog."

"What kind of dog?" Miriam asked, as he left them, but her mother said, "Never mind. We got to get going."

For hours then, they walked the city; her mother's high heels made it difficult for Miriam to hold her hand and keep up with her long strides. Her mother kept pulling her along, now and then yanking her. The sidewalks were crowded; people rushing by kept jostling her. There were bright jagged patches of sky overhead between the buildings and, down below, shadows as deep as night. An old woman in a baggy sweater and ripped scarves put her trembling hand out to touch her. "Stop gawking and keep moving," her mother snapped. "Can't you go faster?"

All afternoon, they went from factory to factory, up tiny elevators or dank stairwells, into high-ceilinged rooms—some full of rows of women at sewing machines that made the place hum like a giant beehive, some full of presses and mangles loud as gunfire. Everywhere there was the smell of smoke and leather. The men who worked the big machines seemed half-asleep; they looked up without seeing Miriam as she hurried past. At each place, she would sit in an outer office watching her mother through the glass as she talked with this or that man, sometimes laughing, sometimes arguing. At some point at each place her mother and the man would turn around and look through the glass at Miriam, and the man would shake his head or nod as if somehow the sight of the little girl had made some kind of point, or hadn't.

Finally they came to a massive plate-glass window of a toy store on a busy avenue. Her mother said, "Stay here. Don't move. I'll be right back," then disappeared into a doorway down the block. Miriam had never seen so many toys, too many to count: giant dollhouses, and dolls in the most stunning clothes, and tea sets with flowers delicately painted on the outside of the cups, the saucers rimmed with gold. An electric train ran through a winter village. She watched the small pistons shunting, and a thread of steam curl from the smokestack. There were thumb-sized children skating on a pond, a fire station with a fire truck out front complete with ladder and hose, and a schoolhouse with dime-sized windows in which she could see children at tiny desks. The village of a storybook, a fairy-tale village.

Then her own face was floating in the glass as lights went out in the store beyond the window; she was looking through a ghostly version of her own face at the toys and realized that it was dark outside. It was night now. How long had she been standing here, lost in dreams? It was night and people were hurrying by in both directions. She was dizzied by the hats and overcoats flowing all around her, the angry traffic. Where had her mother gone? Which building had she entered? She was crying now, bawling, a great big baby, too terrified to care, then out of nowhere her mother spun her around and knelt and, shaking her by the shoulders, said, "Didn't I tell you not to go anywhere? Can't you just do what I tell you?"

Mr. Perez appeared behind her. He was holding the hand of a little dark-skinned girl who was staring wide-eyed at Miriam. She had thick black hair that tumbled down over the shoulders of her coat.

"This is Juanita, Miriam," her mother said. "Juanita, Mr. Perez's little girl."

Miriam wiped her eyes and nose and, still whimpering, shook the girl's hand. The girl kept staring at her, saying nothing.

"We're going to take you kids to a show," Mr. Perez said to Miriam. Then he said something to Juanita in Spanish. His eye closed as he smiled. "What do you say to that? A real Broadway show."

MIRIAM HAD NEVER been inside an actual theater before. Although many shows previewed in Boston before coming to New York, and Bubbie would often talk about taking Miriam to see them, she was always either too busy or too tired, or Zaydie would say they couldn't afford it. But here she was. The enormous ceiling and the countless rows of seats, the balconies and the towering red curtains on the gigantic stage—she forgot all about the day and all that had happened.

She barely noticed that her mother and Mr. Perez had left them there by themselves until she heard Jaunita whimpering.

"Shhhh," Miriam said, touching the girl's arm, which the girl then pulled away. "The show is starting. You can't cry here. It isn't allowed."

When the orchestra hit the first note of the overture, Miriam forgot all about Juanita. She forgot everything but the world of *Show Boat:* the "Cotton Blossom," that floating dream of song and dance, and the love of the riverboat gambler Gaylord for Magnolia, the captain's daughter, and Julie, the singer with a secret past, her Negro mother, and the tragedy that follows, the tragedy and self-sacrifice, all of the bad things converted by the perfect bodies of the beautiful performers, by the voices and the dancing, into a truer life, a richer life—a life that while the show went on obliterated every trace of what went on outside the theater, destroyed it just as surely as the sun destroyed the image of her mother in the window of the train.

• • • • • • •

Scene III

• • • • • • •

After New York, there was outside and there was inside. Outside, there was the mess of too many things Miriam didn't understand, there was divorce and a stylish and scary mother who was hardly ever at home, and grandparents who were kind but old and helpless, and a sad and mostly absent father. But now inside, there was Miss Julie, the mulatto singer who somehow made the mess outside seem far away. Julie would wear only formal dresses and her best shoes. She wouldn't raise her voice, and she wouldn't cry; Julie possessed a sorrowful and mysterious air. Julie would never play in the streets, she wouldn't know from hopscotch or four square or any other game. When they'd ask her why she was this way, all Miss Julie would do was sigh, hold the back of one hand to her forehead and turn away. No one would smile knowingly at Julie or embarrass her with everything she didn't know—she had lived and seen too much for that. Oh, some of the narrow-minded in her world might scorn her. Let them. In doing so, they only showed how small their hearts were, how little they understood about the terrible things that happen to the purest of the pure. Julie wouldn't cry or whine, even when those around her said it wasn't natural—acting like an adult the way she did, a goyishe adult at that, and not a girl. Julie wouldn't cry even when teased about her father, for Julie had no father. She would sigh and walk away. All day long she'd hum "Can't Help Lovin' Dat Man" or "Ol' Man River." "What's wrong with you?" they'd ask. "Why don't you act your age? Stop acting like some crazy adult. It isn't right." But Julie knew right from wrong. No one knew the difference more surely than Julie.

THE RABBI'S OFFICE was in the basement of the synagogue. It was windowless and sunk in books, old books, thick books, a mound of them open on his desk, their onionskin pages torn or dog-eared. The walls were lined with shelves piled high with folders and more books, the linoleum floor awash in notebooks and loose sheets of paper. The black-suited rabbi had a long yellowish beard, and his skin, too, was yellow, the color of parchment, his fingertips ink-smudged. The office smelled of mildew and chickpeas. Directly behind him, two large wooden replicas of the tablets of the Ten Commandments, one in Hebrew, one in English, were hung side by side above a bookcase.

When she entered, he gathered up the books on the chair beside his desk and placed them on the floor. "Come," he said, "come, sit." He patted the seat, leaving a palm print in the dust.

As she stepped carefully to the seat, she looked down at her shoes, their sheen already dulling.

He said her mother wanted him to talk with her. The rabbi's face was kind but grave. He was smiling at her, his dark eyes narrowing to nearly nothing, but his smile was full of sadness. This was the first time she had ever spoken with Rabbi Mandelbaum, the first time she'd ever stepped foot inside his office. What did he know about her? What had he been told about the trip to New York City?

Suddenly she was back in the train watching her mother's face adrift there in the window, looking down at her account books while warehouses and vacant lots passed through it. She saw her mother disappearing into a golden elevator with a man Miriam didn't know—what was his name, Perez? What kind of name was that? And then she saw Miss Julie in the blazing stage lights, looking out into the audience, looking out at Miriam herself, at Miriam and no one else, and singing about all the feelings Miriam didn't know she felt until she heard them in Miss Julie's voice. If there was sorrow in that voice, there was beauty, too, and the beauty made the sorrow seem weightless, ghostly, like her mother's face.

"My mother?" she said. "You mean my stepmother. My poor mother is dead."

"Dead?"

"Dead, yes." She sighed. "But it's better this way; she isn't Jewish."

"Isn't Jewish? How can this be?"

"She's Negro," she said.

"Negro?"

"Yes, Negro. I'm mulatto; I'm an outcast, Rabbi. My father . . ."

"But Miriam, dear . . ."

"And my name's not Miriam, it's Julie."

"This is nonsense."

"No, Rabbi," she said. "It's tragic. It's a tragic story. I'm going to die a drunkard."

"Tragic? Die a drunkard?" He took his glasses off and rubbed his eyes. "What do you know from tragic?"

He told her that she had her whole life to be tragic in; who knew, God forbid, what lay in wait? If God didn't want us to be children when we were children, we'd have all been born in suits and dresses; we would be born with bills and mortgages and children of our own. Even Jael, little one, even Sarah, Rachel, Esther, and Ruth, they were all little girls once. It's a sin not to enjoy the gifts God gives.

"Rabbi, excuse me, but what about Eve?"

"Eve? What about Eve?"

"She was never a girl, was she?"

"And look what happened? Look at the trouble she caused! From playing with dolls, she didn't suffer!"

They stared at each other for a long moment. Then his face grew solemn. One hand stroked his beard while the other pointed over his shoulder to the tablets above his head. "Darling, can you read?"

"Of course I can," she said. "I can read. The English anyway."

"Okay, then, dear, read commandment number seven. Read it out loud to me. Read it slowly, darling, please."

She looked up at the tablets and in her best elocutionary voice intoned, "Thou shalt not commit adultery."

Her eyes grew wide. "Adultery? It's a sin to act like an adult?"

"See," the rabbi interrupted, nodding wisely. "This is no joke. This is serious business."

"I'm an adulterer?" She couldn't speak. Tears welled in her eyes.

"Don't worry, Miriam. Go home, God will forgive you. Of this I'm sure. Go home and get out of these fancy clothes and play with your friends. God will forgive you if you play like the Jewish child you are."

But Miriam wasn't listening because Miriam wasn't Miriam—she was Julie, the singer, the mulatto, the drunkard, and now, best of all, the adulterer.

"SO, MIRIAM, THE rabbi, what did he say?" Zaydie asked that night at dinner.

Miriam didn't answer. She was studying her plate of food.

"Miriam," he asked again, "the rabbi, what did he tell you?"

"Are you speaking to me, Grandpapa?"

"A moment ago I was," he said, lifting a teacup to his lips. "Now, I'm not so sure. Rabbi Mandelbaum, what did he say?"

"I'm an adulterer," she declared.

Slowly he put the teacup down. Hands over her mouth, Bubbie seemed to be coughing.

"Hoo boy," he said. "That's some big deal."

"Yes," she said, wiping her mouth primly with a napkin. "An actual sin."

"You're telling me," he said. "But, kindele, what are you gonna do about it?"

"What's to do?" she answered sadly. "I've been adulterating for so long now, I'm not sure I can stop."

"Oh no," he said, "I don't mean the sin. The golem I'm talking about. Didn't the rabbi tell you about the golem?"

"No," she said. "Who's the golem?"

"He comes for the little girl adulterers, and he spits on them and they grow old right before his eyes."

"Older than you, Zaydie?" she asked.

"Older than me and Bubbie combined," he said. "And all they grow is bald, like a cue ball bald, I'm telling you, and they shrink, and wrinkle, and fall apart like a rag, a shmatta, a good-for-nothing sack of ash. They don't remember nothing. They don't see nothing. They mumble to themselves they don't know what, until all their teeth fall out but one, and that one has a toothache. "

"Can't anything be done to help them?"

"No," he shakes his head. "No, once the golem's spit is on you, you're his forever. Go cry to him and all you'll hear is 'Miss such-a-hurry-to-grow-up, you want to be an adult? Be an adult!' "

She pictured a windowless dark apartment where nobody lived except her and the golem and the women mannequins, all naked and bald and smoking phantom cigarettes. She pictured the golem laughing and cursing in her mother's voice, as she herself got older and older, walking with a cane first, then a walker, then using a wheelchair, and then confined to bed, a shriveled dummy, shriveled and bald, too weak to roll over or call for help, only the golem's wicked "You want to be an adult, be an adult" in her ears.

"Is it too late for me, Zaydie?"

"I don't know," he said. "But, kindele, go to your room and get your dolls out and play with them. Golem will be looking for Miss Julie, not for Miriam. Play with your dolls and maybe he won't know she's here."

She ran to her room and got down only her baby dolls. She made the baby dolls ga ga and goo goo each other; she made her voice as young as possible, even younger than Baby Snooks, as far away from tragedy as Mattapan was from Manhattan, as the golem was from the little girl she'd try from now on to be.

To make amends, Miriam believed it wouldn't be enough for her to be a child; she had to be the best child, the most considerate and beautiful child. She had to be liked by everyone, especially the sad, the disappointed, the vexed. She'd befriend the outcasts and the scorned. When Zaydie's butcher shop went belly-up, and her mother's business nearly faltered, she ate less so there'd be more food for others. She cleaned not just her own room but Zaydie and Bubbie's room as well. She cleaned rooms that didn't need cleaning. And it was during this time of penance and restitution that she tried to befriend Sylvie, the fat girl across the street.

Sylvie had red hair, a dimpled chin, and cheeks that jiggled madly when she talked. She had what Bubbie called a "foul mouth." She was mean to everyone, as if she wanted everyone to hate her. But Miriam would get through to her. Miriam would change her for the better. Playing with Sylvie would show the golem how good Miriam could be, how far she had come since her days as an adulteress.

She knocked on Sylvie's door one Saturday. "What do you want?" Sylvie's mother asked.

When Miriam said, "I was wondering if Sylvie could come to my house this afternoon to play," Sylvie's mother said, "You mean it? Seriously?"

Her mother pushed Sylvie out the door. "You girls have fun," she said. "Sylvie, play as long as you like."

They went to Miriam's house and played dolls in her room. Miriam wanted to play family—mother feeding child, mother cuddling child, mother pushing child on swing. Sylvie just watched scowling. Then Miriam suggested they play *Dancing Lady,* the new musical picture show that had just come to Boston, the new poster for which had just been slapped up on the billboard over Fleischman's Bakery, and she danced her husband and wife dolls around and around.

Then Sylvie said, "Hey, I have an idea. Let's play divorce," and grabbing the dolls from Miriam, she banged the husband's and wife's heads together, and then picked up the baby, and cried, "Wah wah wah." Then she picked up the husband again, saying, "Shut up, you little runt, you, or I'll tear your whiney little head off."

"Why do you want to do that?" Miriam asked.

"Nobody's ever played with you like that, I bet. And where's your dopey father anyway? Probably screwin' some dirty tramp."

As if it belonged to someone else, Miriam's fist flew at Sylvie, hitting her square in the jaw. Sylvie fell back and scrambled to her feet. "You're just like everybody else," she screamed, and Miriam felt the floor shake as Sylvie, crying, lumbered down the stairs and out the door.

Later that night, Sylvie's mother called, asking to speak with Miriam. Fearing the worst, Miriam picked up the phone. Sylvie's mother wanted to know if Sylvie could come play with her again tomorrow afternoon. Miriam broke another commandment, one she hoped the golem didn't care so much about: "Sorry," she said. "I'm busy tomorrow. Maybe next week."

Scene IV

As the next few years went by, the world became larger and smaller at the same time. The kitchen radio was always on in the evenings, even during dinner. They listened amazed and angry to Father Coughlin and his anti-Semitic ravings, or to the news in Europe, which was worsening by the day. All through the broadcasts, Zaydie would mutter, "Bastards, no-good goy bastards." But Miriam couldn't bear to think about Hitler or inflation or the fall of Europe or what now was being blamed on the Jews. Every day more and more strangers from the old country were arriving in the neighborhood. There were stories of persecutions reminiscent of the Middle Ages, of biblical times. The world seemed fearfully unsettled. She was seventeen years old, a senior at the Girls' Latin School in Dorchester. She had ambitions, dreams. Like her friends, she wanted to marry and raise wonderful children, but she also fantasized about the theater, of a life of teaching and acting, singing and dancing. And yet who knew, what with war coming (everybody said it was), what sacrifices would be demanded of her, what obstacles she'd have to overcome. And as if all that weren't bad enough, there was her speech-interpretation teacher to deal with—Gertrude Pinkerton, the faculty adviser to the drama club to which no girl could be admitted without her say-so.

Mrs. Pinkerton was a widow, and even though her husband, Curtis, had passed away ten years ago, she still dressed only in black to commemorate what she called their "matrimonial alliance." He had been, she told the girls, a poor relation of the Pinkertons of the Pinkerton National Detective Agency, so they should think of her, their teacher, "as the national detective, the enforcer, if you will, of the beauties of the English language." She had a long face and narrow nose, and her mouth seemed fixed in a permanent look of being put upon, her thin lips turned down somehow even when she smiled, which she hardly ever did. She greeted her class each morning by reminding them of how many days were left in the school calendar and how many days were left till she herself could finally, thank God, retire. "Good morning, ladies," she would say, as they all took their seats. "You'll all be pleased to know that there are one hundred and fifty-six days remaining in the school year and, by my calculations, eight hundred and seventy-four days, give or take a day of sick leave, remaining in my illustrious career patrolling these august halls of learning."

She had divided up the class into three separate choruses based, she said, on the heft and resonance of their voices.

Miriam thought it an odd coincidence, though, that she had put all the gentile girls into one chorus, all the Jewish girls into another, and all the Irish and Italian girls into a third. She had then divided each chorus further into high and low voices. Those with high-pitched voices she referred to as "light," and those with low-pitched voices she referred to as "dark." Then she had assigned the choruses a poem to learn each week; whichever chorus gave the best performance, which meant striking the proper balance between dark and light, earned the privilege of giving a public recitation to the entire school at Friday-morning assembly and, best of all, the opportunity to join the drama club.

At the beginning of each class, Mrs. Pinkerton would have the entire class read out loud from the introduction to their poetry anthology to remind them of what a poem was. "Louder, ladies," she would say, "louder, enunciate, please, no mumbling, expectorate the 'spuds' from your mouth, please." They would read together about how "verse originates in intense emotion which finds no ready release in activity; this pent-up feeling quickens one's sense of rhythm and expresses itself in a manner of speech adequate both to the thought and to the pulsing motion of that thought, and this in turn enables one to gain a heightened power that allows him to substitute 'unity' for frustration, routine, and the boredom that comes from emotional poverty."

Each morning, as Miriam read these sentences, she would imagine that she was reading instead about the stage and all the feelings that a song released. She longed to perform publicly, to sing in front of others. She had a good voice, everyone said so. And everyone said, too, that she was beautiful—her big blue eyes so eager to take in everything around her, her hair done up in the latest fashion, her blond curls and waves swept up off her high forehead, her figure made more slim and rounded by the crepe day dresses she loved to wear, by the drapes and folds that followed her sleek shape. Movie-star good looks, they said. Shirley Temple, all grown up. She noticed how men mostly, but even some women, would look at her now when she was passing in the street.

But it was already spring, and her chorus, "the Jewesses," as Mrs. Pinkerton called them, had never once, not once, been chosen to recite to the school. Only the gentile girls' chorus, week in, week out, seemed able to strike that je ne sais quoi balance between light and dark, to articulate the just-right tonal subtleties of Tennyson or Longfellow, Shakespeare or Keats. The Irish, Italian, and Jewish girls were either too light or too dark. It was unfortunate; it wasn't their fault, Mrs. Pinkerton consoled them. "The tang of steerage," she said, her mouth grimacing into a smile, still clung to their intonations.

So Miriam formed a drama club of her own with a few girls from the neighborhood. They met once a week on the weekends, each week at a different member's house. Each week a different member would choose the songs they'd sing or the scenes they'd stage. Sometimes they told jokes, and sometimes if the space was large enough they danced. But no one, not ever, was allowed to bring in poems to recite. That was Miriam's one restriction. Mrs. Pinkerton had given her enough of that. She named the club the Mattapan-Manhattan Club—the Manhattan Club for short.

One Saturday in May at Dottie's house off Talbot Square, they were learning a new hit song, "Polka Dots and Moonbeams," when a boy showed up—his name was Frankie Kaufman, and he was Dottie's cousin. Twenty-two years old, he was tall, stoop-shouldered, and shy, with thick dark hair falling over his forehead, which he combed back with his fingers. He couldn't take his eyes off Miriam. She loved how it felt being watched that way, being listened to. Dottie, too, saw how he was watching Miriam and asked if she would stay for supper. And before Miriam knew it, she and Frankie were sitting side by side at the dinner table, and he was telling her about his life, his dreams, how he lived with his mother and sister, that his father had died a few years back, and that he was determined someday to travel the world, then go to college and become a teacher. He wasn't sure, though, if any of that would happen anytime soon, not with the war coming, and besides, his little sister was crippled from a childhood accident, and his mother's eyesight was failing, and right now he was all they had—so he was working in a downtown shoe store.

Miriam could already see herself as Mrs. Frankie Kaufman; Miriam Kaufman—the name had a nice ring to it. It startled her how quickly the dream took shape, the two of them in

Watertown or Newton, maybe Natick—Mrs. Kaufman, the teacher's wife. She could do theater on the weekends or maybe teach it in the schools. And they would travel in the summers till the children came. With a father like that, what brains they'd have!

So lost was she in that imagined life, she hardly heard a word he said.

After dinner, Dottie put "Polka Dots and Moonbeams" back on the gramophone. Frankie asked Miriam to dance. A great dancer he wasn't, but she could teach him. When the song was over, he asked Dottie to play the song again, and they kept dancing. Miriam sang as they danced. Every now and then, Frankie would tilt his head back and look at her adoringly as she sang: he couldn't believe his great good luck—that's what his look said. Dottie and her parents watched them. Miriam could feel the envy they must be feeling, watching her glide back and forth across the floor, which could have been a stage, with Frankie, too, now singing "Polka dots and moonbeams around a pug nosed dream."

Now it was summer, and if she wasn't working at the store for her mother, she was with Frankie. The Mattapan-Manhattan Club dissolved without Miriam's intensity holding it together. Sometimes it disturbed her to think how easily her passion for Frankie had displaced her passion for the stage. But they went to shows and pictures. He loved the theater as much as she did. He loved to dance, and he loved it when she sang to him. Once they were married, and Frankie had found a teaching job worthy of his smarts, maybe then she would return to school.

In the meantime, she worried. They'd been dating for several months and still he hadn't introduced her to his mother and sister. By then, he'd met her mother and Zaydie and Bubbie. She'd even brought him to the butcher shop in Brighton where her father worked, though he was too busy to come out from behind the counter. He had apologized and smiled shyly and said, as he always did, that soon they'd get together. Everyone of course approved. Her mother said he was a catch; well, what she said was "he's a safe catch," whatever that meant. But whenever Miriam asked him when he was going to bring her home to meet his family, he would hem and haw. It just wasn't the right time, or someone was sick, or there was too much going on. What was he afraid of? She knew he had fallen for her. No one, he said, could make him laugh as she could; she was so beautiful, so lively, what had he done to deserve her? She was just the kind of girl any fellow would want to marry. Meeting his mother and sister was the next logical step. It was embarrassing to have to tell her friends and family it hadn't happened yet. They'd raise an eyebrow: they'd say, I'm sure he has his reasons, but she could tell they thought something was up.

One Saturday they were walking home after seeing *The Philadelphia Story,* when she stopped suddenly and threw her arms around his neck and kissed him. Right there on the street in front of everyone, she kissed him. People stepped aside as they passed, some smiling, some clapping. "Go get her, tiger," someone called. Arms still around his neck she said, "Frankie, sweetheart, it's time to introduce me to your mother."

"You don't understand, Miriam," he said, running a hand through his thick black hair. "It's complicated."

"It doesn't have to be," she said.

"My mother, my sister, they're not ready. They need more time."

"For what? What's to get used to with someone like me?"

"It's not you," he said, sighing.

"Then what it is?" She pulled away from him. "Are you ashamed of me?"

"Ashamed of you?" He shook his head. He held her face between his hands. "No, honey, I just . . . I, okay, listen" (she'd never seen him look so full of sorrow), "how about next Saturday? I'm working at the store, but I'll get away for lunch. How does that sound?"

"Good," she said. "I know they'll love me."

MRS. KAUFMAN WAS wearing a bathrobe and tattered slippers when they arrived. She was a tall woman with a long neck and unkempt hair that made her look as if she'd just come in out of a windstorm. Her gaunt face looked confused, like a sleepwalker who'd suddenly awakened and had no idea where she was. Her eyes were magnified and warped by the thickest lenses Miriam had ever seen (they looked like insect eyes seen under a microscope). Miriam had to keep herself from staring. Mrs. Kaufman apologized for not having gotten dressed. Looking vaguely in Miriam's direction, she said, "Ronnie wouldn't let me sleep all night, what with the pain in her legs, and the moaning, and then this morning the buckle on her leg brace snapped off; I called Bernstein to come fix it; he said he couldn't get here till this afternoon. I said, what am I supposed to do, carry her to the toilet? I can hardly make it there myself. Anyway, you don't need to know all this. Come in, come in." Mrs. Kaufman led them through the dark apartment to the sunroom, her fingers brushing the walls, the backs of chairs, the tables, feeling her way along.

Ronnie was seated on the couch, a massive metal brace on one leg, the other spindly and bowed, extending from her house dress. Her legs looked stiff and lifeless, like the legs of the unused naked mannequins in the back of Tula's shop. Two black canes, one on either side of her, were propped like sentries against the couch. Her frizzy brown hair made her face seem longer and thinner than it was. She could have been Miriam's age, or older, maybe even older than Frankie.

Like a small girl, though, she said, "Frankie, sit next to me, sit with me, Frankie."

As Miriam took her seat, Ronnie smiled a smile that had nothing friendly in it.

"So, Frankie," Mrs. Kaufman said, "this Miriam's a real beauty."

Frankie's eyes twitched; he looked down at his feet, as if he'd just been scolded.

"Oh for God's sake," Mrs. Kaufman said, "I almost forgot."

And with remarkable agility and quickness Mrs. Kaufman brought a tea set on a silver tray from the breakfront to the coffee table, and set out the saucers, the cups, the napkins, the spoons. She filled each cup to just below the brim, and then returned the tea pot to the tray, and the tray to its exact spot on the breakfront.

With no expression in her voice or face, her mouth hardly moving, Ronnie asked, "Do you read books?"

"Yes," Miriam said, louder than she meant to. "I love to read. I read novels, plays, magazines. How about you?"

"Not since the accident," Ronnie said. "The words hop around too much. Frankie reads to me. Frankie reads a lot of books."

"Frankie's quite the reader," Mrs. Kaufman added. "A regular professor. Graduated from Boston Latin top of his class. He wants to go to college, isn't that right, Frankie?"

Frankie said, "Sure, Ma."

"His father was smart, too, a real brain. He got degrees, don't ask, an MA, a BA, and if he hadn't gotten sick, he'd have been a doctor, may he rest in peace."

Mrs. Kaufman smiled in Miriam's vicinity, saying, "What does your father do, dear, if you don't mind my asking?"

"He's in the meat business."

"Oh," she laughed, "another professional."

"Excuse me?"

"An MD," she said. "Meat Dealer!"

Frankie excused himself and disappeared into the dark apartment.

"You know, Miriam," Mrs. Kaufman's voice grew solemn. "My Frankie, he has a lot of plans, big plans. He wants to travel the world. He wants to go to Africa and work with the schvartzas, can you imagine that? Did you know he speaks four languages?"

No, she didn't.

"Yes, and he works so hard, my poor son, and you know we're no walk in the park, Ronnie and me."

"I can't even walk in the park," Ronnie said.

"Shush, Ronnie," said Mrs. Kaufman. She sipped her tea, staring at Miriam, right into her eyes. For the first time, Miriam felt looked at. Assessed.

"Think you're special?"

"Excuse me?" Miriam said.

Leaning forward, Mrs. Kaufman hissed, "You'll end up like the rest of us, you wait and see. You'll be just the same, miss high and mighty. Think you can waltz right in here and take whatever you want, like we don't matter, like . . ."

Suddenly Frankie was back, and Mrs. Kaufman sat back, wiping something from her cheek. "More tea?" she said, smiling at her son.

No, Frankie was due back at the store, they had to run. Ronnie wanted to know when he'd be home, so they could finish reading *Little Women.* Beth is going to die, isn't she? And what about Jo and the professor, would they get married? What time would he be home, what time exactly? He wasn't going out again tonight, was he?

Mrs. Kaufman walked them to the door, touching the furniture and wall along the way. She said again how beautiful Miriam was, a regular Betty Grable. That Frankie, he's got great taste in girls. She said next time she won't be so tired. Next time, she'll dress up proper. They'll kibitz longer.

Miriam said she couldn't wait.

FRANKIE'S LETTER CAME a few days later. She was a wonderful girl, the best girl he'd ever met, but he had too much responsibility as it was, and she was so young—she deserved a better life than he could give her.

She was not surprised. She pretended to be crushed. For days afterward, she cried, she moped, but there was also a pleasure in the crying and the moping, in being the spurned one, the rejected one. She could think that she hadn't done anything wrong, that she had nothing to regret. It was just his family, just fate. It wasn't in the cards. He loved her; he still loved her, maybe now more than ever. She could probably get him back, if she really wanted to. But she wouldn't do that, no, because she knew deep down that it was best for him and for his family if she gave him up. When you came right down to it, she hadn't really been rejected. No, she had sacrificed her happiness for his well-being, the way Miss Julie had. Miss Julie, her guardian angel. It had been years since she had thought of her. Now she could sing "Can't help lovin' dat man" and feel, sadly yet sweetly, too, as if everything had happened for the best.

In a few weeks, only the thought of Ronnie and Mrs.

Kaufman troubled her. She'd be daydreaming her bittersweet dreams of the life she might have had with Frankie, the places they'd have gone, the important work she might have helped him with—she'd be imagining their story as a musical, a tragic musical like *Show Boat,* dreaming of them as a pair of star-crossed lovers, singing their way from scene to scene—when suddenly *they* would appear, the crippled girl and the blind mother. Suddenly she'd feel looked at and hated. She'd think, how long before I can forget them, once and for all?

Scene V

Without Frankie in the picture, and high school over, Miriam went to work full-time for Tula. She thought of college from time to time, but she knew that Bubbie and Zaydie couldn't possibly afford to send her, and her mother wouldn't. Her mother said that for someone like Miriam college was just a high-priced mixer, a place to snare a husband. And it was just as likely she would find a good catch here at home as on a fancy campus. "You can buy a bra at Filene's Basement or at Macy's. But either way it's still a bra." Tula herself hadn't even finished high school, and she had done all right, "Especially once I got that nonsense with your father over with." When Miriam said she wanted to become a teacher, a theater teacher, and maybe even someday perform, her mother scoffed, "And I want to be Mrs. Rockefeller." Miriam could pursue these pipe dreams if she wanted to, but she'd have to do it on her own nickel.

Miriam had to learn, like Tula had, the hard way, that there were no free lunches.

A full-time working girl: Miriam liked the sound of that. And anyway, it wouldn't be forever. And maybe, for once, her mother would recognize her talent—her go-getter attitude, her effervescence, her easy way with people. To her surprise, the work itself became a kind of performance, one in which she got to play her mother. She pretended to be the woman she had watched in secret all those years ago, the one whom all the customers admired, the confident businesswoman, the fashion maven, the friendly, knowing counselor who always had a good word for everyone, who knew just what to say to make even the plainest woman feel oh so stylish ("Darling, it's stunning how the fabric hugs your hips!" "Oh, the color's gorgeous, perfect for your complexion!" "This will get a rise out of him, dear, believe me—your husband sees you in this, he won't say he's too tired to go dancing!"). She played her mother, and the store did well. Business, in fact, was never better. And the better the store did, the more time Tula spent in New York City. Miriam had to hire a friend from high school to help out during the holiday season.

She even made some innovations. Tula had such confidence in the merchandise and her own ability to sell anything to anyone that she had never paid much attention to the window displays. But Miriam experimented with the mannequins and began, especially in the weeks leading up to Christmas, to arrange them in various domestic scenes: a mother in a stunning evening gown (was she about to go out for the evening?) bending over to kiss what looked to be a little baby in a crib; a woman in casual slacks and sweater serving appetizers in front of a hearth in which silver foil pretended to be fire; two women in satin pajamas, a mother and daughter, or sisters maybe, chatting warmly in a kitchen, cigarettes in long holders rising to their lips. Customers, new and old alike, remarked upon how clever the displays were, how quaint. Tula either said nothing to her, or wryly offered, "If I liked that sort of thing, I'd say you did it very well."

Well, after all these years, what did Miriam expect? The job would not be forever. She had bigger fish to fry. And in the meantime, whether her mother noticed or not, she'd work at playing Tula better than Tula played herself.

EARLY IN 1941, a friend knew a friend whose brother Miriam just had to meet. His name was Hank, Hank Gold, though everybody called him Curly because of his thick wavy head of jet black hair. He was as tall as Cary Grant and just as handsome. He was strong, too, and Miriam could feel his muscles under his jacket when she took his arm as he walked her to the car. He said he got them from hauling meat all day in his father's slaughterhouse.

They went to the Mayfair for dinner and dancing. She loved the soft lights on the dance floor, how while they danced in the dimness he was half-imagined as well as half-perceived.

His image changed from moment to moment, from tall dark stranger to entrepreneur, from dapper Dan, the dangerous bounder, to family man, a protector and provider. She imagined the kind of woman he imagined he was dancing with, a woman with blond hair and a slim figure, a mysterious beauty. He was something on the dance floor, smooth and confident, a Jewish Fred Astaire. They sang and danced all that first night. When they left the Mayfair, they were already a couple.

That very night she began the scrapbook she would keep right up to their wedding day. She called it *ROMANCE: Curly and Miriam.* The title page bore an epigraph from Abraham Lincoln: "Love is an agreeable passion: love is sometimes stronger than death, and folks that love know it." Agreeable passion: Miriam liked the sound of that, passion that behaved well, passion with manners. Everything in her world right now seemed agreeable.

Over the next few months, they saw every show that came to Boston: *Banjo Eyes* with Eddie Cantor, *Arsenic and Old Lace, My Sister Eileen, Claudia, Dream It Music.* She saved each and every playbill, every ticket, and every menu of every place they went afterward to eat. She'd paste them in her book and underneath write a line or two: "He's darling," or "Curly picked me up at 7, I didn't get home till after 2 (Ahem!!)," or "What a naughty boy he is sometimes." Every now and then she'd show Curly the scrapbook, and he began to add a line or two himself.

After their third date, she wrote, "We had dinner at the

Latin Quarter, and spent the evening there. I told Curly about my dreams, college and the stage, and he said he had plans, too, of starting his own business, and when he hit it big, his lucky wife (I wonder who that will be!) would live on easy street and do whatever she wanted. He's so adorable." A few days later, he added underneath her entry, "Miriam said she was afraid of love." After the next date, a formal dance in honor of a friend's engagement, she pasted the ribbon that was tied to a "gorgeous orchid" under which she wrote, "It poured cats and dogs this night." And under that, he later wrote, "Miriam admits she loves me."

FIVE WEEKS AFTER Pearl Harbor, early in 1942, Curly was inducted into the army. He was sent to Camp Devens for training. He mailed her an official-looking "release form." It read:

> Safety First Guarantee:
>
> This certifies, that I, the undersigned female, about to enjoy sexual intercourse with ___________, am of the lawful age of consent, am in my right mind, and not under the influence of any drug or narcotic. Neither does he have to use any force, threats, or promises to influence me.
>
> I am in no fear of him whatsoever; do not expect or want to marry him; don't know whether he is married or not, and don't care. I am not asleep or drunk, and am entering into this relation with him because I love it and want it as much as he does,

and if I receive the satisfaction I expect, I am very willing to play an early return engagement.

Furthermore, I agree never to appear as a witness against him or to prosecute under the Mann White Slave Act.

Signed before jumping into bed, this ____ day of ______, 19___.

She pasted the release form in the scrapbook, under which she wrote: "Is he fresh!!!!" Under that, he later wrote, "She said no."

Now she couldn't think past Curly, and their uncertain future, where he'd be sent and when. She couldn't think past any moment with him, any date. She loved him, she was certain of that, but it troubled her how annoyingly persistent he could be at the end of every date. With Zaydie and Bubbie sleeping down the hall, she and Curly would be necking in the parlor, and he'd want to do it. He'd lean back and say how much he loved her and who knew what tomorrow would bring. His hands were strong and confident, hers shy and uncertain. At some point, smiling that smile she never liked, that knowing smile, he'd take her hand and guide it where he wanted it to go. She felt like a schoolgirl, like an idiot, and she grew angry at him for making her feel so "inexperienced," even if she was. Why wasn't there a college for this?

No, no she couldn't, not till they were married. Yes, she loved him but what if Zaydie or Bubbie found them? Yes, she knew she was now eighteen and old enough. But what if she got pregnant? He'd lose all respect for her, and anyway, they had their whole life before them. When they were married, when they had their own apartment, their own bed, then it would be perfect, they'd give each other everything they'd ever dreamed of.

But he wouldn't stop pestering her, leaning against her, his body tense, his hand now cupping her breast, pressing on it; in the pressure of it, she could feel the even greater pressure he was holding back, the force of what he wouldn't do but could, if he wanted to—of everything she wasn't strong enough to stop. It hardly had to do with him at all, that force, that pressure, it was just some "blind thing" inside him that took control of him, and in the grip of it, he could have been any man, a stranger, and she just the body of a woman, any woman, no better than a naked mannequin.

He'd stop; he'd always stop. But some day they'd be married, and there'd be no reason to stop, and then what? She told herself by that time it would all be different, she'd want what he wanted and always when and how he wanted it; marriage would turn her into the woman he imagined she would be, and that she wanted to be for his sake. But when she tried to picture married life, the day to day of it, she pictured them as a couple always out with others, dancing and singing, as if on stage, Fred and Ginger in stunning clothes, and she pictured children and the houses they would live in, and the bright rooms within those houses, and even the tasteful furnishings in every nook and cranny. She could see herself and Curly everywhere except in the marriage bed—in the bedroom, there were no lights on; that room was dark, and the bed was darker, too dark for her to picture the naked bodies tangled in the sheets.

BECAUSE SHE FELT so much relief when he was sent to Camp Lee, Virginia, she wrote him every day about how much she missed him and couldn't wait till they were back in each other's arms. She tried not to think about how easy it was to love him when he wasn't there. She never liked the old saw that absence makes the heart grow fonder—didn't it seem to say that love was some sort of fantasy? But what she felt now in his absence was the opposite of fantasy—his being gone didn't create some imaginary scenario—it gave her the room she needed to see him as he was, and to see herself more truly as a fiancée pining for her gorgeous soldier boy. His being gone enabled her to see them as the couple they would become when they were married. "Love," she wrote one night in the scrapbook, "is like a script you can't hold too close to your eyes if you really want to read it. Otherwise you can't make out what the words are saying."

THREE WEEKS LATER, he came home on furlough. One night, they went to the Balinese Room with her cousins Charlie and Irene. Miriam had to work late that evening, so she was meeting them there. She had told Curly to order her a drink. When he had asked what kind she wanted, she had said, "Surprise me."

Miriam was dead tired by the time she got to the restaurant, which was crowded and noisy. It had been a long day; maybe it was all the bad news from Europe, but everyone who came through the shop that day was on edge and quarrelsome. She'd been showing clothes all day, catering to the needs and whims of every customer, sometimes for hours at a time, and yet by day's end she hadn't sold a thing. She was hungry, frustrated, and she needed a drink.

Curly, Charlie, and Irene were seated at a table just off the dance floor. The waitress was standing next to Curly, taking drink orders. Miriam waited before approaching the table. She wanted to see what drink he thought she'd like. She watched her soldier boy make small talk with her cousins. The three of them were laughing like old friends. God, how they adored him—everybody did, and not just for his good looks but also for his charm, his easy way with people. He was smart and had a head for business and big dreams, too, as big as hers—wait till the war is over and he gets out from underneath his father's thumb! Nothing would stop the two of them! She bought a pack of Marlboros from the cigarette girl. When she reached the table, the waitress had returned with the drinks. She placed a beer in front of Curly, a gin and tonic in front of Irene, and a vodka gimlet in front of Charlie.

When he saw her, Curly stood and held up his drink, and said, "Here's to the girl in high heel shoes / who spends my money and drinks my booze; / who crawls into bed and snuggles up tight / and crosses her legs and says good night."

Irene and Charlie laughed. Curly said, "Hey honey," and tried to kiss her but she leaned away.

"Where's my drink?" she asked.

"Your drink?" he said. "Oh, Jeez, hon," he said. "I forgot in all the hubbub I was supposed to order for you."

"What you were going to order for me?" she asked, now holding an unlit cigarette, waiting for him to light it.

"I don't know," he said, not noticing the cigarette. "I really haven't had a chance to think about it—what did you want?"

"I wanted you to order me a drink."

"I'm sorry, sweetheart," he said. "We were kibitzing and I just . . ."

"A little consideration, is that too much to ask?" She threw the cigarette down on the table. "I've been on my feet all day. I'm tired."

"Give him a break, Miriam," Charlie said. "The boy's only home for a weekend. You got your whole life to nag him."

"Stay out of this, Charlie."

"Okay," Irene said, "we get it. You're tired. You want a drink. So, order a drink already."

"I want Curly to order it for me."

"Jesus!" Irene said.

"Calm down, honey," Curly said. "I'll get it, I'll get it."

"Since when did you become so hoity-toity," Charlie said. "You'd think your father was a Rockefeller and not a butcher."

"Don't start with me about my father. You leave my father out of this."

She got up and ran crying to the bathroom. Irene followed after to see what she could do. Curly ordered her a drink, a Bloody Mary—it was waiting for her when she returned.

"Sweetheart," he said as he stood and put his arm around her, her eyes still red from crying. "I'm sorry, I should've remembered. Here's your drink."

When she saw the Bloody Mary, she laughed. "Well, I guess I deserve it. Just a bad day at the office. Thank God it's over now."

"I'll drink to that," Curly said.

"Bloody Mary," she said, laughing again. "You're such a kidder." She ruffled his hair and pulled out a cigarette. By the time it reached her lips he was already holding the match flame up to it.

THAT NIGHT, SHE pasted a postcard picture of the Balinese Room in the scrapbook. She wrote, "Spent the evening with my family; Curly and I danced all night. Food not so good." He wrote, "Miriam had a fracas with family."

CURLY SIGNED THEM up to perform in the Camp Lee couples talent show. Miriam flew down to Virginia for the performance. It was almost like being in show business. One minute she was home in Boston in the middle of winter, and the next she was in Virginia, on stage in high heels, fishnet tights, and a barmaid getup with a short black skirt. Behind her stood Curly and two other men dressed to the nines, replete with top hat and cane. And as she sang "Embraceable You," the men behind her twirled their canes in unison as if they were rifles. Her voice sounded low and sultry. Her lips fondled and clung to every note, as if reluctant to let it go, to let it disappear into the next note and the next. Left to right, she stepped across the stage, singing, "Just one look at you . . ." while, right to left, the ham-handed Maurice Chevaliers marched behind her, canes tipping the top hats down over their eyes. Then Curly broke out of line and took her in his arms, his beautiful wife-to-be, and sang, "Come to papa," and as he dipped her down and smoothly drew her up, they sang together, My sweet embraceable you. The soldiers in the audience went wild.

FINALLY THEY MARRIED and she moved to Charleston where he was stationed. Just shy of nineteen, and here she was in the Deep South, far from everything she knew, in a small apartment on the base. This would be the first meal she would cook for him. Her neighbor, Gloria, a friendly big-boned redhead with enormous breasts, had given her a recipe that she called "Southern Spaghetti." Miriam spent all afternoon getting ready—cleaning, buying groceries, preparing the sauce. She borrowed from Gloria a checkered tablecloth and two tall candleholders. And though she and Curly didn't drink much, she bought a bottle of expensive red wine to mark the occasion. When he got home, the room resembled a Parisian bistro on the left bank of the Seine.

Here they were at last, facing each other across the wobbly

metal table, in flickering candlelight. She held up her wine-glass, watching him intently as he lifted the first forkful of the first home-cooked dinner of their married life.

He tasted. "What kind of shit is this," he blurted out. The glass flew from her hand, and he ducked. What the . . . ?! They looked at each other. For a moment, they had no idea who it was they saw.

MARRIED HOUSING UNITS were more like bunkers than apartments—theirs was a studio, with a fold-out couch, a floor lamp, one table to dine on with two chairs, and a galley kitchen with a staticky Philco radio on the counter and a porthole window above the kitchen sink. It was so small there was nowhere not to be in someone's way. And the walls were thin, and every night, in the next apartment, every single night, Gloria and her husband, Tommy, went at it longer and louder than Miriam thought was possible. She felt judged by every shriek and groan, by the bed board banging on and on against the wall, on the other side of which Miriam and Curly lay unable to sleep after doing or not doing whatever it was they did or didn't do.

MIRIAM COULDN'T DENY it anymore: she loved best the appearance she and Curly made together. He was so good-looking, especially in uniform, that she felt more beautiful beside him. She loved the outward show of married life, the handsome and adoring newlyweds with their future all before them. He was a good man, too, a family man. She loved all that about him. Sex was the least of it; sex had nothing to do with devotion or beauty or being seen. Sex was the opposite of being looked at as they made an entrance. It was like dancing in the dark when no one's watching, performing a play to an empty theater. Sex confused and scared her. Why? She couldn't say, and if she could, who would she have said it to? It was just that there was something he expected from her, something she was supposed to know—he wouldn't tell her what it was, and she wouldn't ask, even though she hated not knowing it, and hated the advantage she imagined he must have felt knowing and not telling her what it was she was supposed to do and when and how often she was supposed to do it. That he never complained only made it worse, because she sensed his disappointment, his resentment, sensed it in the dutiful way he held her for a moment afterward before he turned away, and they would lie there back-to-back, listening to the inexhaustible couple on the other side of the wall. At least *Curly* got what he wanted, even if it wasn't perfect. He got some relief, and if truth be told maybe she did, too, since for a night or two afterward he wouldn't pester her. But then she'd feel the pressure building up again and then, just when all she wanted was to go to sleep herself, he'd touch her in that way, and if she didn't reciprocate he'd get moody and sullen. She knew what he was thinking: she's like a little girl, a child; she's not a woman (like the one next door), not a real woman. Angrily, she'd give him what he wanted. She'd do it. She'd get it over with. Fast and furious.

He shipped out to the Philippines onboard the USS *Dakota.* The war ended just as he reached the Pacific theater. He saw dead bodies everywhere but no action. Onboard the warship, soldiers and nurses were hopping in the sack day and night, right under the noses of their commanding officers who pretended not to know. In his letters, Curly referred to the nurses as "tomatoes" ("a real tomato") and to the most beautiful of them as "tomato puree." He'd describe their faces and their figures, not, he said, to make her jealous, but only so she'd see how much he loved her—that, even as tempted as he was, and lonely, he'd be true to her because he loved her so much, and anyway, next to her, these gals were "just a bunch of old potato pickers." They couldn't hold a candle to his wife.

He also wrote about the suffering everywhere, the devastation. After what he'd witnessed of the war, he said he'd never complain of anything again. Like Lou Gehrig, he wrote, he was the luckiest man on the face of this earth.

Writing to Curly, and reading his letters, Miriam felt the fog of confused feeling lift again and she grew hopeful about the life ahead, the children they would have—they'd be wonderful parents. Wasn't that what sex was for? Wasn't that why they had married in the first place? Yes, she missed him; the world was a dangerous and terrible place, but they would be each other's safe haven. They would be each other's shelter from the storm. All she wanted to do was hold him. All she wanted to do was make him happy. She pledged to dedicate her life to that.

ACT
II

Scene I

Just after the war, they're posing for a photograph at a cousin's wedding. It's a photograph of Curly's family. His brother and sister-in-law and two of his older sisters and their husbands sit at a table while Miriam and Curly and his younger sister and her husband stand behind them. The table is round, and there's a white carnation in the middle of it, surrounded by empty plates, drinks, water glasses, and the crumpled napkins of those who have had to stand for the picture.

The youngest sister's husband is an inveterate womanizer. Only a week or so before this wedding, he was away on business, and his wife called his hotel room at one a.m. and a woman answered. Not long after this picture's taken, sometime in the next few months, she'll file for divorce. This is, in fact, the last family occasion he attends, the last picture he appears in.

Curly's oldest sister has two daughters, both of them mildly retarded.

The brother-in-law sitting at the table is looking to his left at his beautiful wife, who's looking out at the photographer. He adores his wife, but he drinks too much. And she's just about had it. A few years earlier, after some vague business venture went belly-up, he became a hairdresser, a profession associated with homosexuals, with "faygelas." That he is good at cutting hair only increases his sense of having lost his manhood, having failed his family. A faygela with a family he can't support—what could be worse? His wife has threatened to leave him if he doesn't quit the boozing. He doesn't, but before she has the chance to leave him, he drops dead of a heart attack. This, too, is his last picture with the family.

Curly still works for his father and brother in the slaughterhouse, working for peanuts, bubkes, and it drives Miriam crazy how he places loyalty to them over loyalty to her and the family they're trying to have, a loyalty, she's quick to add, his brother and father don't return. The old man is practically retired while the older brother spends most of his time in Florida with his wealthy friends, playing golf, relaxing while Curly works like a dog, running the slaughterhouse day in, day out, seven days a week. And yet he doesn't earn enough to buy a pair of slippers, much less, God forbid, a trip somewhere. What about her plans, or his? What happened to Easy Street?

None of this, of course, is evident as they pose for the camera. Everyone is smiling out at the photographer. The men sport tuxedos; the women, evening gowns. Miriam's hair is marcelled in a thick wave that gathers without breaking down the right side of her face. The other women all have perms. Everyone looks the way they've always dreamed of looking. Somewhere in the ballroom a band is playing " 'S Wonderful" while the happy newlywed couple dances the first dance. But this family, these people, stand here not so much to celebrate the cousin who's getting married but their enduring faith in the glamorous trappings of success. In the moment of the picture, they are what they pretend to be. And no one more so than Miriam, who smiles the widest, her mouth opening as if to suck in all the happiness around her.

Scene II

The first child was a girl with brown hair and gray eyes. Miriam couldn't bring herself to settle on a name. It wasn't because she wanted a unique name, a name unlike anybody else's, a name as special as she knew the child would be. She couldn't name the baby because she didn't think the baby would live. Despite the doctor's assurances that she was perfectly healthy, she couldn't believe something that small and helpless could survive. Why name a child that wouldn't live? A named baby would be a grief magnet; nameless, there'd be less to mourn. Or maybe it was easier to mourn preemptively, to mourn in advance, a nameless baby, so when the loss came she'd be ready for it. The grief would already be behind her. Even after she brought the girl home, she would not name her. She would not name her because the baby slept so much. She slept through the night. She slept most of the day. What a good baby, her friends said, so little bother. But it worried her how much the baby slept. The doctor said, "Enjoy, get some rest; you're lucky she isn't fussy."

But she couldn't rest; she kept going to the girl's crib to make sure she was breathing. The quiet at night was always too quiet; the quiet kept her listening. Then one night the baby cried. Relieved, Miriam rushed to the crib. But when the baby wouldn't take the bottle, and wasn't wet, and wouldn't calm down, Miriam grew alarmed again. She walked the baby from room to room, patting it on the back, shushing it, sometimes singing "People Will Say We're in Love" from *Oklahoma* or "You'll Never Walk Alone" from *Carousel.* She tried one shoulder then the other. She sat with the baby in her lap, against her breast; she lay down with the baby on the couch in the living room. But nothing worked. It was one a.m. and the baby was crying; the baby was crying at two a.m., at three, at four, when Curly got up and dressed. As he left, he kissed Miriam on the cheek and said that if the crying continued she should maybe call the doctor. Big help he is. Now it was just her and the wailing baby in the new apartment they moved to when they found out she was pregnant. One moment she was scared that something was really wrong; the next moment she was frustrated, then angry, then thinking she should slam the baby's head against the wall and at least then she'd know why she was crying.

It wasn't till nine a.m. that the baby went back to sleep. Julie, Miriam told herself, as she lay down at last, we'll call her Julie.

Right from the start, Julie was a quiet child and (Miriam had to admit it) a little standoffish. And three years later, when Ethan, the moody redhead, came along, with his tantrums and his attention-grabbing ways (weren't his first words "me" and "mine"?), Julie grew even more withdrawn and cooler. Oh, she had friends, lots of friends, and the little girl she turned into when her friends were over—affectionate, talkative, eager to please—bore no resemblance to the girl she was at home with just the family. Aloof, not contrary, Julie would shrug and mumble, "I guess," whenever Miriam would ask her if she wanted to play a board game or cook together. But it was never fun because the girl just sleepwalked through the play. It was as if she agreed to almost anything Miriam proposed so as not to disappoint her mother. And yet the more Miriam tried to keep her interested, the more distant the girl became. Sometimes she found herself begging Julie to get more involved, to pay attention. "Come on Julie," she'd say, "play with me, like this, come on, it's fun." But Julie would just look at her as if Miriam were the child, the needy one, begging for attention, and Julie the too-busy mother.

So Miriam backed off. She learned to admire Julie's self-possession, her focus. She came to appreciate, if not entirely enjoy, seeing Julie, often for hours at a time, on the floor of her room with all her books spread out before her, so engrossed in reading, happily in a world of her own. That self-sufficiency, though, drove her little brother crazy. Ethan always wanted

Julie to play with him, or at least watch him play with his truck or his toy soldiers, and when she wouldn't so much as look up from the book, he'd pinch or poke her, and when that didn't work he'd hurl himself into her lap, getting between her and the book, and say, like Thumper in *Bambi,* "Whatcha doin'?" She'd finally cry out, "Leave me alone," and run to her room and slam the door. After a while, he stopped asking her to play and went straight for the poking and pinching, just to annoy her.

"Honey, you're gonna ruin your eyes, the way you read so much," Miriam would say, or "Play with your brother for a change," but Julie just ignored her and kept reading. It scared Miriam how much Julie read, though she bragged to her friends and family all the time about what a reader her daughter was, a brilliant girl, a real professor.

But then with Sam, "the baby," Julie, six years old now, was completely different. Julie couldn't leave Sam alone. Miriam would find her sometimes in the middle of the night at Sam's crib, fussing with his little blanket, or just looking at him. She wanted to hold him, be the one to give him the bottle, or change his diaper, or just play with him for hours on the floor. Sometimes, in the morning, or at bedtime, while Miriam sat with Sam in the big rocking chair beside his crib, Julie would get into her lap, and then Ethan, who couldn't bear to miss out on anything, would climb up, too, and with Julie holding the bottle for Sam, and Ethan sucking his thumb, the four of them would rock together while Miriam sang "Lullaby of Broadway." At such times, half-asleep, Miriam would think, "Someone should take a picture of this, what a picture we'd make," and then falling asleep as she rocked her little ones happily she wouldn't think of anything at all.

Scene III

In 1956, with help from Curly's father, they bought a small two-story Victorian on a cul-de-sac in Allston. They put down thick shag carpets throughout the two floors of their new home and new black-and-white checkered linoleum in the kitchen and bathrooms. Miriam chose an Oriental motif for the furnishings and fixtures—orange paper lanterns instead of lamps, wallpaper showing Chinese farmers in rice paddies, or shirtless and barefooted rickshaw drivers pulling rickshaws behind them, their faces invisible under the broad-brimmed hats they wore. In the living room, she hung lithographs of Parisian scenes—couples walking arm in arm down narrow cobbled streets, across the Place de la Concorde, along the Champs-Élysée. She lined the mantel over the fireplace they never used with figurines of peasant men and women—one swinging a scythe, one sowing seeds, one driving a team of plow horses. Over the twin beds in the master bedroom, she put up big bright posters from her favorite musicals: *South Pacific, Oklahoma, Annie Get Your Gun.* Over her dressing table, she hung a photograph from *Show Boat,* one showing Miss Julie holding her arms out imploringly toward the audience—Miriam imagined Julie was singing "Can't Help Lovin' Dat Man." The bedroom didn't get much light, and the posters brightened it, and made it seem larger than it was. In the bathroom, for old time's sake, she hung a framed poster of Fanny Brice at the *Follies.* In the foyer, beside the coatrack, she hung a painting of London's Tower Bridge, partially obscured by fog. She loved the international flavor of the unpredictable decorations. Inside the house, you'd never guess you were in Allston.

MIRIAM HIRED A sixty-year-old black maid named Melba Bradford to clean for them twice a month. Melba had a round body and thin legs; her graying frizzy hair was pulled straight back into a tight bun. She had a large mole on her right cheek that Miriam had to work hard not to look at. All Miriam knew about her was that she lived in Mattapan not far from where Miriam herself grew up. She arrived at eight on Fridays, and left at five. She never wanted to be fed. She never spoke. She worked nonstop with a blank expression on her face, took her money without a word of thanks, and left. And while Miriam felt uncomfortable around her—there was something Miriam found menacing about her silence, something judgmental or put-upon, although she couldn't quite say how or why she felt that way—she nonetheless adored how nice the house looked after Melba cleaned it. She loved the bracing tang of cleanser in the air, the shiny figurines and vases, the glistening Formica, the polished breakfront, and the streaks left in the carpet by the vacuum cleaner. Every other Friday evening, Miriam felt as if the house was once again brand-new, never lived in, poised for the life that she was meant to live. She recommended Melba, whom she referred to as her "girl," to all her friends and family. She couldn't say enough good things about her girl—her girl, who was reliable and clean and never shilly-shallied.

One Friday, Julie (out of school with a head cold) was in the kitchen eating lunch with Miriam while Melba, on all fours, scrubbed the linoleum, a pail of soapy water beside her. Out of the blue, as if she'd noticed Melba for the first time, Julie said, "Mrs. Bradford, it's lunchtime, don't you want to eat with us?"

Melba never looked up, just went on scrubbing the floor. Miriam shushed Julie. "Just eat," she said, "so Melba can finish up in here."

Later, after Melba left, Miriam told Julie to leave Melba alone and let her do her job. "And don't call her Mrs. Bradford, honey. Mr. and Mrs. we use with neighbors and Mommy and Daddy's friends. You call Melba, Melba, okay? That's what her name is."

THEIR NEIGHBOR DOWN the street, Sigrid Rosenberg, showed up one afternoon to welcome Miriam to the neighborhood. Sigrid was a short woman with a pageboy haircut that gave her broad face and small mouth a pixieish air, like a middle-aged, slightly overweight Peter Pan. She wore a floral house dress with long sleeves even when the weather was warm. She lived by herself. She spoke with a faint German accent. She nodded approvingly at everything that Miriam had done to the house. Everything, she said, was "interesting, so very interesting."

"So drab before," she said, as they sat at the kitchen table, the two of them smoking. "Mrs. Gould, the widow, she didn't care about how things looked; she really let the place run down. Who can blame her though, given everything she went through, and then, you know, what happened to her husband, I'm sure they told you."

"No," Miriam said. "No one told me anything. The realtor said Mrs. Gould had just gotten too old to care for herself. That's why the family put the house up for sale."

"The two of them," Sigrid said, sighing, her right hand resting on the cuff of her left sleeve, "like me, survivors, though I don't know from what camp, one of the Polish ones I think. Anyway, he worked in Zelda's Bakery, near the synagogue. Not a friendly man, just quiet, minded his own business, didn't bother anybody, and didn't want to be bothered, either. One day, just like any other day, he comes home after work except he hasn't even taken off his apron, still covered in flour and powdered sugar all over his hair and face, and he hangs himself in the cellar. No note, no nothing, just dead, caput."

"Oh goodness," Miriam said. "The poor woman."

Sigrid lit another cigarette even though the first one was still burning in the ashtray. She smiled more widely now, as if she'd proven something, though Miriam couldn't say what it was.

"That's how it is sometimes," she said. "Too much to remember, you can't sleep, not even with the pills; what you won't do to sleep—you have no idea. Anything not to think about how stupid it is you're here, just you and no one else. Only you, but not your husband, not your brilliant son or daughter. Just you. What's the good of that? What could that possibly mean?"

She was smiling at Miriam as she stubbed out the half-smoked cigarette and said, "I should be going. The house—may you live and be well here! It's so wonderful to have some little ones in the neighborhood again."

Miriam sat at the kitchen table for a long time after Sigrid left and tried not to think about what she had said. She tried not to think about poor Mrs. Gould and her dead husband and what all of them, Sigrid included, had suffered during the war. She wanted to push the thoughts away, but they felt, just then, immovable. She looked at the kitchen; she tried to feel the stable weight of the house around her. Surely nothing like what had happened to Sigrid and the Goulds, so far away in time, in another world, would happen here. Surely the new house would be her haven, her safe place. But she couldn't shake the feeling that somehow Sigrid had tainted that. How could she keep herself from remembering this conversation?

Sitting there amid her decorations and designs, she felt exposed, found out, as if a window she wanted to keep shut had been suddenly thrown open and anything now might blow in.

From that day on, she tried to be busy and not available whenever Sigrid called. She never told the family what had happened in the cellar. And she herself never stepped foot down there.

Scene IV

At ages seven and four, the boys still wet the bed. Most mornings, they came downstairs to their parents' room where Ethan would get in bed next to Curly while Sam would slip into the crack between the two twin beds. Every now and then, not often, they'd find their parents in the same bed, and something in the way they lay there tangled together told them not to enter, and they returned to the damp sheets upstairs. On those mornings, there was an indefinable sadness in the house; the rooms grew spacious with loneliness. They didn't know how or why. Their mother moved as in a daze to get them dressed, to make them breakfast; she was distracted, elsewhere, moving in slow motion, trudging it seemed across a foreign land, a desert, as if, if she paused even for a moment, she would collapse and die. Their father looked somehow defeated, like a center fielder who started running in at the crack of the ball, then realized too late that he'd gone the wrong way and could only watch as the ball flew over his head, beyond the outstretched glove. Mornings were like that when the boys found them in the same bed, although it happened less and less often. And then they almost never found them in the same bed. And almost anytime they wanted, whether they wet the bed or not, Ethan could get in next to Curly, and Sam could slip into the crack between the mattresses.

Scene V

Of the three children, only Julie wanted to go to summer camp. The boys were too young and besides both were bed wetters. But Julie couldn't wait to go to Camp Winnipesaukee where several of her friends were going, and of course unlike her friends, she wanted to go for the entire eight-week session. Of course she boarded the bus happily, without a tear, without a wave good-bye—and of course she seldom wrote and when she did it was just to Sam, and when visiting day came four weeks later, and Miriam and Curly drove the three hours up to see her, what did she do as she came down the path with the other campers, all of whom when they saw their parents ran to greet them—what did Julie do? She smiled and waved and then ran right past them with another girl who wanted to introduce her to *her* parents whom Julie, of course, was happy, even eager, to meet.

Scene VI

In the summertime for the next few years, on the rare Saturdays when Curly wasn't needed at the slaughterhouse, he'd take the family to the beach.

They'd carry their beach bags full of toys and towels over the hot sand to the middle of a mass of bodies. In the far distance where the shore curved sharply eastward out into the water, they could see the bright white roller coaster from the amusement park rise above the grassy dunes. All around them they could hear the tiny buzzing of thousands of transistor radios—"Young at Heart" on one side, and on the other "Hound Dog" or "Fly Me to the Moon." They could hear children squealing in the surf and on the shore among the glistening teenage boys and girls parading back and forth. Overhead, contrails of jets too high to see would scratch a razor-thin white line across the sky, and slower planes closer to the ground would pass pulling banners advertising tires and restaurants.

Everywhere, too, the odor of coconut oil and French fries, salt and sand. Everywhere laughter and small talk. Summertime, Miriam sang to herself, and the livin' is easy.

Ethan would show Sam how to build a sand castle, which meant Ethan played with the pail and shovel while Sam looked on. Eventually, of course, Sam would want to do more than watch, and Miriam would have to get up and tell Ethan to share. He would stomp off in a huff, but sooner or later (usually sooner) he'd return and the boys would play together. Miriam would then lie back down next to Curly, her leg brushing his or his hers while men, even those with women, would look down admiringly at Miriam's sleek figure, and women, even those with men, would glance at Curly's chiseled frame.

The day was spacious, with nothing to do except lie there and be noticed while you noticed others. And yet at the end of it how tired they always were, but tired without the crankiness they often felt at home in the evenings, tired in a good way, a happily spent way.

On the drive home they'd stop at the Clam Shack on the bay and eat a huge bucket of steamed clams. Sometimes they'd surprise the boys and pull into the drive-in movie theater just past the shipyard, so close to the Baker's factory that the car would fill with the fragrance of chocolate. Miriam loved how excitedly the boys would tumble from the car and run to the playground where other kids were playing while she and Curly would settle in, her head against his shoulder, his arm around her, and watch *Carousel* or *Guys and Dolls* or, her new favorite,

The Best Things in Life Are Free—Curly holding Miriam as she sang along to "Lucky in Love," or "Button Up Your Overcoat," the two of them even singing together, "Take good care of yourself, you belong to me."

Some days it was so easy to be happy it just broke her heart.

Scene VII

To keep her company while she cooked, she put *My Fair Lady* on the record player. The show had come through Boston a year ago, and she had been there at opening night. Curly of course, as always, was too tired to go. She went solo, the only one of her friends who went without her husband. There was Stanley and Dottie, and Harry and Gissy, and her, poor Miriam. She couldn't really blame Curly, she knew that—after all, he was at the slaughterhouse by five each morning, and for the past year he'd been mostly working seven days a week. Someday, he said, all the hard work would pay off; he always promised that when he struck out on his own, they'd be living on easy street. Miriam was beginning to wonder. She tried to stay positive. She told herself that when their ship came in, they'd look back fondly on this time of struggle; they'd see it as the character-building phase of their relationship, like Eliza Doolittle's years on the street, selling flowers, before Henry Higgins, the man of her dreams, turns her into the lady she was destined to become. Maybe, from the pinnacle of her future success, she'd see these years as the "good old days." But right now, she couldn't help but resent how hard Curly had to work and how little he got back in return. She tried not to blame him, but she could and did blame his father and his brother—God, how they took advantage of him—and sometimes, she couldn't help herself, she blamed Curly for his lack of nerve, his inability to stand up for himself. But when she asked him about it, he called it love and respect. Where would he be without his father? How could he disobey his father? Didn't his father give them the down payment for the house? It was like talking to a wall.

But all of that vanished utterly when she sang along to "I've Grown Accustomed to Her Face." While she sang, life itself became a musical in which everybody in the end got just what they deserved. She played the album over and over, and one day, after the third or fourth time, as she lifted the arm off the record to reset it, she heard Ethan singing from the next room. He was singing the same song; while Sam looked on, he was on the floor banging two trucks together as he sang, "I was supremely independent and content before we met. Surely I could always . . ." Barely eight and he sang like a little Eddie Fisher. She couldn't believe her ears.

When Curly got home, she had Ethan sing for him, and tired as he was, even he acknowledged that the kid was good. Very good. Miriam was already plotting her next move. Ethan would have to learn to tap dance; he'd need acting lessons.

He'd need coaching, direction. She wouldn't be able to do this by herself.

SHE FOUND HIM a teacher. His name was Stuart Foster. His studio was on the second floor of an office building in downtown Boston, and every Saturday morning and Wednesday night she took Ethan there. Every Saturday morning and Wednesday night, Ethan didn't want to go. They fought. She sometimes had to drag him kicking and screaming to the car. She didn't care if he hated it; he had too much talent not to go. And someday he would thank her. Someday he would appreciate everything she did for his sake. Sometimes she would hear herself yelling at the boy and shudder at how much she sounded like her mother. But for Ethan's sake she would shake off the feeling and not relent, because in her heart of hearts she knew that she was not her mother. She believed in Ethan. She wasn't leaving her child for someone else to raise while she went gallivanting off to New York City. She'd never do a thing like that. This, she told herself, this was what a mother was, what a mother did. So every Saturday morning and Wednesday night they went, always, even during the summers. Sam and Julie would watch them go. They would watch them fight and go. They sang, too, but thank God not as well as Ethan.

MIRIAM'S FATHER'S HAIR was still jet black and combed straight back over his head. His hair was the hair of Brylcreem ads, shiny and full, though the youthful sheen and fullness only made his wrinkled face seem that much older. The kids stared at his hair every Sunday when they visited him in the living room of his shadowy apartment, while behind him and down a long, dark hallway his new wife puttered in the kitchen. She never turned around; she never came out to say hello. She was nothing but a stooped back in a bright kitchen down a dark hallway. They stared at the old man's young man's hair while their mother nattered on about the week, her plans for Ethan, who'd said what about him. The children noticed how odd her voice got when she talked to her father. Her voice got all . . . they didn't know, they couldn't really describe it . . . soft? girlish? somehow too eager to please? She sounded like kids in school with teachers they were afraid of. But what they were hearing wasn't exactly fear. It was more like the teacher had asked a question and he was looking around the room for someone to answer it, and she had her hand raised, she was waving it in front of him, she was pleading, Me, Me, Me, but he was looking past her, he'd rather hear from someone else for a change, someone not so eager.

The old man just went on smiling and nodding, saying nothing, until finally toward the end of every visit she would say, Ethan, sing something for your Grandpa Maury, sing "Mom-e-le" for Grandpa Maury, and Ethan would glare at her as if to say, why do I have to do your dirty work? Then he slowly stood and sang. His voice was so beautiful. Even Ethan knew it. And while he sang, he forgot about his anger at being asked to sing.

When Ethan finished, the old man smiled and nodded. Miriam went on chattering. The kids fidgeted. They stared. Time stopped. Each Sunday, every Sunday, from one to three, time stopped, and every Sunday they were certain it would never start again. Leaving the dark apartment was like leaving a movie theater—the sun in their eyes too sudden and too bright, it took a moment to get used to it. On the ride home they'd complain, asking why did she make them come? Why can't they stay home, he never talks and he's creepy, and . . . "Enough already," she'd say, in her normal voice now, her rushed, I-can't-do-everything-by-myself voice. "You'll go because you have to. Because I said so."

Scene VIII

Zaydie died of a massive coronary in 1957. Without consulting Miriam, Tula put Bubbie in a nursing home. Miriam didn't like the idea one bit, but when she called Tula to complain, Tula shut her up. She said that unless Miriam could afford to pay for live-in help, or could take Bubbie into her own home and look after her herself, she should mind her own business.

"What is it with you?" Miriam asked. "Why have you always been so hard on her, on everyone? She's your mother, for God's sake."

"What do you know about my mother, or me?" Tula shot back.

"All she ever wanted for you was your happiness?"

"My happiness?" Tula said, laughing. "Wanted me out of the house is what she wanted—fifteen years old, I'm still a girl, a child, and she marries me to that—that butcher? That's a mother?"

When Miriam said nothing, Tula went on, "Do you have any idea what that was like—we're hardly off the boat, and I'm a girl one minute and a butcher's wife the next? And why—because they couldn't afford me? Too many mouths to feed? Is that all I was to them, a mouth to feed?"

"I didn't know," Miriam said. "I didn't realize . . ."

"Everything," Tula interrupted, "everything I've made of myself I made in spite of her, in spite of them. Don't lecture me about who I owe what to. Mother, my ass."

What could Miriam say? What else didn't she know about? Who were these people she spent her childhood with? What was she supposed to do now, knowing this?

Even after Tula repeated, "Mother, my ass" and hung up, Miriam sat there, saying nothing, holding the dead phone to her ear.

ONLY A FEW months later, Tula, only fifty-eight years old, collapsed in the store. She couldn't speak; she couldn't walk. At the hospital, the doctor told Miriam that the stroke might leave some residual deficit, but there was no reason to think she wouldn't recover most of her motor skills. By the time Miriam arrived, her mother already had recovered enough to grunt and wail but not yet to articulate even the simplest word. Half of her face was frozen but Miriam could tell from the other half that she was furious. Whenever the nurse entered the room, her mother growled; Miriam thought she was saying keep that bitch away from me. "Mother," Miriam said, "everyone's only trying to help." But her mother refused to listen. She wouldn't leave the IV shunt alone so they had to tie her arms down. It took three nurses to hold her still enough to do this. She wouldn't eat, she wouldn't drink; she thrashed her head from side to side whenever anybody so much as looked in her direction.

Tula seemed to blame them all for everything, the stroke, the slurred speech, the inability to walk; she blamed them all, it seemed, Miriam especially, for being there to see her in such need. It was as if she thought their health had caused her sickness, and so to punish them, to show them all who was boss, she would not cooperate. She wouldn't deign to help them help her.

By the third day, she seemed calmer. When the doctor examined her, she responded to his questions: she touched her fingers, she blinked, she nodded. She also expanded her repertoire of sounds.

At one point she said to Miriam, "I wa . . . I wa . . . I wa . . ."

"What mother?" Miriam asked. "What do you want? Do you want something?"

"I wa . . . wa wa wa," but she couldn't sound it out. She grunted in frustration and turned her head to the tray table beside the bed, toward the pen and paper by the phone.

Miriam handed them to her. Slowly, in a trembling script, she wrote "smoke."

"Smoke?" Miriam asked. "Do you smell smoke?"

She frowned. She wrote, "No, goyishe kop, cigarette!"

Miriam wouldn't buy them for her. "They'll kill you," she said. "You want to die?"

Her mother nodded yes, yes I do, the sooner the better.

SHE HAD JUST gotten home and started dinner when the phone rang. Miriam's heart sank when she heard Sigrid Rosenberg, her neighbor down the street, say, "Miriam, dear, I'm so sorry about your mother."

Miss Gloom and Doom, appearing as always at the first scent of catastrophe. "How nice of you to call," Miriam said. "I'd been meaning to call you, too, but, well, you know . . ."

"Of course, dear," Sigrid said. "Such a terrible time. I know. I don't want to bother you; I just wanted to know how your mother's doing."

"She's coming along, but it's not easy."

"No," Sigrid said, "easy it never is. But your attitude, staying positive, looking at the brighter side—that makes all the difference."

"I'm sure it does."

"So many in the camps," Sigrid went on, "they just gave up, stopped trying, and next thing you know, caput, they're gone. But the fighters . . ."

"Oh, my," Miriam interrupted, "look at the time. I'm running late, and the kids will be home soon."

"Like your mother," Sigrid continued. "I can tell she's a tough one, that one, you wait."

"Yes," Miriam said, "she's a fighter. Always has been, but really Sigrid I have to . . ."

"Family is so, so important, darling. Without it, you're nothing. Take it from me."

"I certainly do," Miriam said.

"Do what?"Sigrid asked.

"I, um, you know, take it from you," Miriam stammered, "take to heart, I mean, what you're saying, and I really appreciate you calling, but I have to get dinner going."

"Such an ordeal," the woman said, "sometimes you have to wonder."

"Well," Miriam said, "I'll give my mother your regards. Thanks so much."

"Don't mention it," Sigrid said, then added, "How's that little one of yours, the blond?"

"Sam?"

"The one who walks around with his shoes untied."

Miriam had no idea what she was talking about. "Why do you ask?" she said.

"Some day he's going to trip and break his skull."

"Okay, well, thanks for calling," Miriam said and hung up before Sigrid had a chance to say another word.

MIRIAM GOT THE kids off to school each morning, then spent the remainder of the day at the hospital managing her mother's care. She forced her to do the physical therapy; she encouraged her, she cajoled her, sometimes she scolded her as one would scold a stubborn child. It was worse than getting Ethan to his music lessons. It was as if their roles had suddenly been reversed, the neglected daughter now the mother, and the mother—always so brusque and independent—now a needy and helpless child. Miriam couldn't see herself as rising heroically (and forgivingly) to the occasion, although she tried. God knows she tried. Day by day, singing to herself "You'll Never Walk Alone," she carried out the task as best she could. Within a month, her mother could speak again, though her words were slurred; she could also walk, though she shuffled unsteadily like a toddler. Her left shoulder never regained feeling, so when Miriam would lose her temper, as she sometimes did, when she'd catch her mother smoking, or complaining or refusing to do anything to help herself, Miriam would hit her not terribly hard, and only there in the shoulder where her mother had no feeling.

One afternoon toward the end of her mother's rehab, Miriam saw a well-dressed man in the dayroom sitting by her mother's chair. He leaned close, their heads nearly touching. As Miriam approached, she noticed they were holding hands. The man rose when he saw her.

"Senorita," he said, smiling, taking her hand and kissing it. "You remember me, of course, your mother's friend, Issa Perez. New York, so many years ago?"

Yes, Miriam remembered. Of course. So good to see him.

He was heavier now and his hair was graying, but he looked

as elegant as ever, a middle-aged Ricky Ricardo. His left eye seemed to wince when he smiled, making his impeccable manners and his poise seem shaky, fragile.

"I see your mother wasn't exaggerating," he said. "You've become quite a beauty. No wonder she's so proud of you."

Proud of her?

"When Tula didn't come to town last month, and didn't call, I wondered. I telephoned the store and they told me what had happened. Your mother didn't want me to come, but I had to see her."

Tula said slowly, haltingly, as if reading from a poorly printed script. "Tell him, Miriam, tell him to go away. To go home to his wife."

"But darling," he said, reaching for her hand, which she pulled away.

"Go home," she repeated. "This isn't me. There's no me here. This," and now she waved her hand over her lap, "this is not me. Go away, all of you."

"Darling," he implored, "sweetheart, you don't mean it."

He turned to Miriam. "Can't you reason with her? She can't just turn her back on me, on all our years together."

Years together? What years? How? Who was he, anyway, this married man? And where was the black-haired daughter, was she, too, part of "this" history they shared, their separate life, or was he as much a stranger to his daughter as Tula was to Miriam? Why should Miriam help him?

He looked stricken. His bottom lip was trembling. Miriam

understood only too well what he was feeling, his helplessness, his pain. She remembered the lobby of the hotel and the chandelier she had to sit beneath for hours while he and her mother disappeared to do who knew what; she remembered the toy store on the avenue at night and all the strangers rushing past her, the terrifying loneliness; she felt in her very nerve ends everything he now would have to do without. She thought of sad Miss Julie, and she felt sorry for the man; she thought of the two-timing riverboat gambler and she hated him. She didn't know whether to sock him or take him in her arms and sing his pain away. All she could do was stand there, dumbfounded.

"Senorita," he said, taking her hand again and kissing it. "I should go now." He handed her a card. "If she changes her mind, please let me know. Be good to her, please, for my sake."

After he left, Miriam and Tula sat in silence for a while, until Tula said that she was tired and wanted to lie down. "Okay, Mother, whatever you want." Mr. Perez's card fell to the floor as Miriam rose. She left it there. She took her mother's arm and helped her up and walked her carefully down the hall to bed.

Scene IX

What an odd child Sam was becoming. So pretty, with his blond curls and big green eyes, that people would stop Miriam on the street and say, Ooo such a beautiful boy, I could eat him up, I could just kill him! But what they didn't know were his quirky needs and habits. With Ethan and Julie, she could go anywhere, do anything. At the beauty parlor, Ethan (for a little while anyway) would thumb through magazines, and Julie, of course, would read her book. But Sam, he couldn't sit still; he'd follow her to the chair and ask what this or that was, what the different combs were for, the different clippers, could he use the electric razor? What's so permanent about a permanent, if it doesn't last? And why does it smell so bad? You couldn't take him to a restaurant or to someone's house for dinner because he wouldn't cut his food—he said eating food cut with a knife gave him a sore throat. He'd jam his fork into a steak and gnaw at it like an animal, like he grew up in a barn. And then there was the fuss he made about his clothes. On school days, he wouldn't leave the house until he'd gotten his shirt tucked in just so. He couldn't bear the thought of the shirt coming loose. She could never tuck it in far enough. After she'd tighten his belt to the last notch, as far as it would go, he'd raise his arms and wail if the shirt pulled out even just a little. It was as if he thought the world would end, as if life itself depended on his shirt staying put. Finally, she or Curly would get so enraged they'd blow up: "For Christ's sake, get out of the house, you crazy kid you, you're gonna drive us nuts." Now that Sam was eight, Miriam decided he should spend his Friday nights at her mother's apartment, to keep her company. The old lady took an interest in the boy that she never seemed to have for either Julie or Ethan. She loved to show him off to all her friends in the building. What a doll, she'd say. Her mood brightened whenever Sam was there.

"Why do I have to go?" Sam would ask. "Why can't Julie or Ethan go?" And Miriam would say, "Because you're her favorite, that's why. It's just one night and she's lonely, and you're going, and that's the end of it."

Every Friday night followed the same routine. For dinner, Tula gave him a steak and baked potato, and a glass of ginger ale. At least she didn't care if he ate his steak with a fork. Then they'd visit her neighbors in the next apartment, Fanny and Gerta, two sisters, identical twins, in their eighties. To Sam, they looked like carbon copies of the Wicked Witch of the West from *The Wizard of Oz:* long nose, spiky chin, and thin lips that, even closed, seemed to be smiling, or just about to. They even dressed in black. The apartment smelled musty, like a cedar closet full of mothballs; there were rugs everywhere, and thick drapes, dim lamps, and stone sculptures of little naked men and women. The three women would smoke and tell the same stories and repeat the same complaints. At some point in the evening, Fanny and Gerta would take turns repeating their favorite Burma-Shave poems from the safe-driving billboards along the highway. One sister would recite the poem, and the other would say, "Burma-Shave."

Don't lose
Your head
To gain a minute
You need your head
Your brains are in it
Burma-Shave

He tried
To cross
As fast train neared
Death didn't draft him
He volunteered
Burma-Shave

Eventually Gerta would bring up the subject of her ex-husband and how selfish and cruel he was.

"No-good bastard," Gerta would say, and Fanny, who had never married, would add, for Sam's benefit, "Pardon her French."

"Empty my bank account," Gerta would continue, "and

walk out on me like that, without a word, not even a note. Not even a telegram."

"Not one bit of explanation," Fanny would offer. "Imagine that!"

"And mine," Sam's grandmother would say, "mine, what a greenhorn, the way he dressed, the way he spoke, and a penny-pincher, you wouldn't believe, and if I wanted to do something with a girlfriend, you know, see a picture or get a drink, he'd get all high-and-mighty. It isn't right for a married woman to be out alone on the town, like a tramp, a regular floozy—and this from a butcher. I couldn't stand it."

"What are you gonna do," one sister would say, and the other would add, "Not a goddamn thing."

Turning to Sam, his grandmother would ruffle his hair and say, "But this little one, what a husband he'll make, that'll be some lucky broad!"

"What a catch," the sisters would say together. "We could eat him up. We could positively kill him."

Then Gerta or Fanny would sigh, and say, "What are you gonna do?"

And getting up to leave, his grandmother would sigh, too, and add, "Not a goddamn thing."

Back in her apartment, with Sam on the couch, and his grandmother in her recliner, a halo of cigarette smoke around her head, they'd watch *Rawhide* and *Gunsmoke,* Sam's favorite TV shows, though halfway through *Gunsmoke* his grandmother would begin to cry. She'd sob, "Issa, Issa," or "My goddamn body," and when he'd ask what's wrong? why's she crying? who's Issa? she'd just keep crying, as if he wasn't there. And then there was what always happened next when the show would end and it was time for bed. He dreaded bedtime because there was only the one bed, so they had to sleep together, and every single night he'd wet the bed. He couldn't help it. He tried not to fall asleep but he always did. And he would wake up to "Oy Gott, oy Gott," as she lifted off the damp nightgown, and made him take off his pajamas, and together, naked, in the dark room they would change the sheets. He couldn't look or not look at the horrible breasts, the enormous overhanging belly, and the flabby legs. When the bed was made, he'd lie down with his back to her, on the far edge of the mattress and wait for morning.

And when morning came, he'd dress and kneel beside the window and look down at the street below, watching for his mother's car. His mother always promised that she'd be there by eleven, but it was often after three before she showed up. For hours he'd watch the cars pass, never breaking his vigil, not responding even when his grandmother would ask him if he wanted something to eat, or did he want to watch cartoons, or what was wrong—why won't he talk, cat got his tongue? He wouldn't talk, he wouldn't turn around. He knew he hurt her feelings, but he didn't know what else to do. By the time his mother appeared, he'd be too eager to get home, and too guilty about his own behavior, to show how furious he was. He'd sit beside Miriam in the car, in silence, while she told him how much good it did her mother to spend time with him. "You're the only one she loves," she'd say. "If it weren't for you, she wouldn't want to live."

Scene X

Ethan's teacher, Stuart, was in his early forties. He was not what Curly would call "a man's man." A little portly but not fat, and always dressed impeccably, in blue blazer and bow tie, he was witty, attentive, courtly. "And how are you today, my dearest," he'd always ask when Miriam arrived. Then he'd take her hand and bow slightly. His voice, so articulate, so refined, reminded her of Mrs. Pinkerton's voice, her high school teacher, though without the snootiness, without the poetry she hated. He knew everything about show business and Broadway, and had even worked with Buddy Greco a few years back, *the* Buddy Greco, one of Miriam's favorite singers. He also played the piano like nobody's business. She loved to watch his delicate and nimble fingers dance across the keys. And best of all, he had a way with Ethan, who would listen to him and never argue, never talk back. And he recognized Ethan's great potential. He said he'd never had a student with talent like Ethan's. Oh, the sky was certainly the limit.

Miriam looked forward to the Saturday and Wednesday lessons. She loved the bright lights of the studio, the musty smell of the place, the mirrors along one wall, and the floor-to-ceiling window that divided the office from the studio, the office where she'd sit and watch in rapture as Stuart taught the kids to "shuffle off to Buffalo" or step/kick/step, or sing a medley of numbers from *Bye Bye Birdie, Carousel,* or *Oklahoma.* Watching Stuart, she felt a new connection to the theater, to show business and Broadway. And the excitement she had felt on that first visit to New York, the grandeur of the stage, the oversized emotions of the songs, the way even the saddest words were changed to joy and pleasure by the perfect voices singing perfect melodies—she felt it all again, with an overpowering freshness. Sometimes, during a dance number, Stuart would ask Miriam to sing along with him, and while she belted out a number from *Pal Joey,* or *Porgy and Bess,* or *Damn Yankees,* a happiness would overtake her, a sense of being right where she belonged, where nothing bad could ever happen.

ETHAN'S FIRST PUBLIC performance was during the intermission of the New England Fashion Show at the Statler Hotel in downtown Boston. Everyone who was anyone, all the muckety-mucks, were there, even Joan Kennedy (Teddy's adorable wife) wearing a smart blue suit dress with a short cropped jacket, accessorized with a pearl necklace and white gloves. Miriam was sitting right behind her, two rows from the stage where, cameras flashing, the stunning models paraded the latest styles, styles her mother would have carried had she not had to sell the business after getting sick. It was like the mannequins had come to life before her, in swing or poodle skirts, and pencil skirts; in dresses with bolero sleeves and Peter Pan collars "softening the neckline" and tapered waists to emphasize what the MC called the "hourglass figures of today's American wife and mother," figures not much smaller than Miriam's, which could still turn a head or two on a good day.

And then Stuart, in an elegant white tuxedo, appeared on stage at a piano, then Ethan followed, in knickers and vest, a baseball cap turned sideways on his head, like one of the Little Rascals from the movies. He was leaning against the piano, arms folded, looking dreamily out at the audience as he sang, "Your smiles, your frowns, / Your ups, your downs, / Are second nature to me now . . ." Oh how everybody looked at her when he was finished, even Joan Kennedy when she realized who Miriam was; they congratulated her for having such a son; how proud she must be, how excited! What's it like, they asked, to raise a budding star?

WHEN ETHAN HAD a new song to learn, he would listen to it on the stereo in the dining room, next to the kitchen, in the early evenings while Miriam made dinner. He'd stand next to the stereo with his eyes closed mouthing the words over and over until he learned them. Then with the sound turned low, so Miriam could hardly hear the music, he'd sing in his pure high, steady voice. Miriam wasn't a bad singer, but she couldn't sing like Ethan. Who could? And she often wondered what it felt like to possess a voice like that, to sing so beautifully, with such emotion. How lucky her child was to have such a gift.

One evening, he was practicing "Over the Rainbow." From the darkened dining room, he sang and sang, and it seemed to Miriam, as steam rose up around her from the big pot of soup she was stirring, that he sang more powerfully than Judy Garland herself, and he was younger than she had been when she had made that recording. When he finished, tears filled her eyes.

"Honey," she said, "That was so beautiful."

As he turned to the stereo to set the arm back at the beginning of the song so he could sing it again, Miriam asked him if he liked that song.

"It's okay," he said. "I like singing it."

"And what do you like about it?"

"I like how it makes me sound sometimes," he said.

"And what's that?" she asked.

"I don't know," he said, "just good. Like when you wish for something that you think you're gonna get."

"When I was a little girl," she said, "that's just what singing was for me. A kind of wishing."

"And did you get what you wished for?"

"Well," she said, stirring the big pot with one hand, waving the steam out of her eyes with the other, "sort of. At least while I was singing."

"Like you were wishing for the song?"

"Something like that. And for the happiness I felt when I would sing."

"Weren't you happy, Ma," he asked, "when you were little?"

She stirred and stirred the soup.

"Weren't you happy, Ma," he asked again.

"Not like you, darling," she said. "I couldn't sing like you. You're lucky. Your wish comes true every time you sing. Remember that next time you cry about not wanting to go to Stuart's."

He placed the needle back at the beginning of the song, and he sang in that beautiful, high, clear voice of his, and as he sang, she stirred and listened.

HALF-DRESSED, THE BOYS were hurriedly slurping up the last of their cereal. There was milk all over the table and little puddles of it on the floor. As always, Curly had left for the slaughterhouse at dawn, before anyone else was up. But his saucepan with dried egg in it was still on the stove, and his unwashed plate sat on the counter beside the sink. Miriam wanted them all out of the house so she could straighten up and get to Stuart's. He had wanted her there early so she could help him work out a new tap dance routine for Ethan. But she was running late, and there were still the boys' beds to deal with, and the kitchen to clean, which now looked like a war zone.

A piece of toast in one hand, her book bag in the other, Julie was heading for the door, leaving behind a trail of crumbs.

"I'll be home late, Ma," she said. "Cheerleading practice. Might miss supper."

"Why should this day be different from any other day," Miriam said. "But eat something more. You can't learn on an empty stomach."

She heard the door slam and Julie's "Yeah yeah yeah" as she went down the front stairs.

"Ethan," she said, "we have Stuart tonight."

"Aw, Ma," he whined, "not again. I don't want to go. I got too much to do, I got a lot on my plate."

"A lot on your plate," she said, "like what?"

"You know, homework, and stuff."

"That'll take you what, fifteen minutes, a half hour at most?"

"Okay," he said, "so it's a small plate. I don't want to go."

"You're going."

"Shit," he said, throwing his napkin down and stomping out.

"Don't use that language with me," she yelled after him, "or I'll tell your father."

Now Sam was leaving. His shoelaces were untied. "Wait," she said. She bent down to tie them.

"Don't touch my laces," he said. "Don't you tie them!"

"What do you mean, don't tie them? If you don't want me to tie them, learn to do it yourself."

"I don't know how," he said. "And I don't like the way you do it. They always come untied at school. And I'm always tripping."

"Get Mrs. Cunningham to tie them," she said.

"Then the kids'll laugh at me."

"So what are you going to do?" she asked. "I can't let you leave with your shoes untied."

"Mrs. Rosenberg," he said.

"Sigrid? Down the street? What about Sigrid?"

"She'll tie them. She said she would."

"When did she say she'd tie them?"

"A while ago, 'cause I told her you didn't know how to."

"Why were you talking to Mrs. Rosenberg?"

"'Cause she saw me walking home from school and said I was going to fall on my head, and that would be it, caput, I'd die, just like that, if I didn't tie my laces, and so she tied them for me, and they didn't come untied until I went to bed."

So now she couldn't tuck in his shirts and couldn't tie his shoelaces. He'd rather have a Holocaust survivor tie his shoelaces than his own mother? Plus, the neighborhood probably thought she neglected her children, and for all she knew maybe they thought she abused them, too. Who knew what crazy ideas that woman would put in Sam's head? And Ethan wouldn't go to Stuart without a fuss, and Julie—Julie was never home.

And then there was Curly to look forward to at the end of the day—angry as ever, full of complaints, wanting to know where Julie was and why Miriam couldn't control her, and why did she have to push Ethan so hard, it wasn't right for a kid to spend so much time singing and dancing with that "faygela" Stuart. "You want him to end up working for your father, too?"

she'd have to say to shut him up. "Think that will make him happy?"

Same routine—morning after morning, night in, night out. The happy family in their happy home.

SHE SPENT MORE and more time at the studio, arriving early, staying late. She'd go on days when Ethan didn't have a lesson. Stuart had such a way with children; one group would be tap dancing while another would be singing. He wrote music; he choreographed dance numbers; he was always busy, always doing a thousand things at once. His energy and exuberance were contagious. After a while, she found herself helping him with his books and making appointments. She had even begun helping him compose and arrange.

One day, during a break, Stuart put his hand on her shoulder. The gentle pressure of it made her blush. There was trust in the pressure, and comfort, an undemanding intimacy she'd never felt before. And the pleasure she felt just then sent a jolt of fear right through her heart.

"Miriam," he said, "you seem a little blue lately. Everything okay?'

"I'm just tired," she said. "You know—the kids, my mother."

"No," he said, "I don't know, being a confirmed bachelor and all."

"Ignorance is bliss," she said. "At least it can seem that way sometimes."

"And Curly? You didn't mention Curly."

"Curly's Curly," she said.

"He's quite a looker, though, that hubby of yours."

"A real man's man," she said. "That's him."

"Well," he said, "this is me; and I was wondering if you'd consider making our 'relationship' official."

"Official?" she asked. "As in making an honest woman out of me?" She blushed again.

"Or me," he said, smiling sheepishly. "I mean coming to work here, being my assistant, what with all the reviews and performances I'm lining up, I could use some help, someone to fill in for me when I'm away, keep the place shipshape and all that. And it wouldn't be such a bad thing for Ethan if you learned the business."

"I'd have to check with Curly," she said. "But I like your proposal."

"Okay then," he said, "let's tie the knot, in a manner of speaking. And Curly can give you away."

"Throw me away is more likely," she said. "But yes, let's do it—so to speak."

CURLY WASN'T CRAZY about the plan.

"We have enough trouble managing," he told her, "without you prancing around with Stuart."

"We could use the money."

"We're doing fine."

"When was the last time we took a trip?"

"Hey, I'm too busy working to pay the bills, to put food on the table."

"What happened to easy street? All our big plans?"

"What are you talking about?"

"Nothing. Never mind. Forget it." She was silent for a moment, then said, "What I mean is, with a little extra, maybe we could go somewhere for a change. Do something. It wouldn't kill us."

"I'm too goddamned tired."

"All our friends go places. They travel everywhere, they go on cruises. Harry and Gissy just got back from Israel. They said it was beautiful. They'd never seen such beauty."

"Hey, listen, we live in the most beautiful country in the world. The Grand Canyon, Las Vegas, the Rocky Mountains—you name it we got it all right here in the US of A."

"So why don't we go to Vegas?"

" 'Cause I don't like to travel."

"Listen, Curly, I'm taking the job, okay? Whether you like it or not."

STUART WAS ALWAYS delighted to see her; he never failed to kiss her cheek. Oh, she knew what he was, what he was saying when he'd refer to himself as "a confirmed bachelor." Even to think the word *homosexual* or *fag* made her blush. Her whole life she'd heard the family, Curly's as well as hers, refer to any man even a little different as a "faygela." He doesn't like baseball?—must be a "faygela"; plays tennis, not football?—"faygela"; loves opera?—"faygela." Ballet?—light in the loafers. If it weren't for Frank Sinatra, they'd think all singers, including Ethan, were "faygelas." Faygelas were everywhere, it seemed, though she herself had never met one, so far as she knew. If Stuart was, big deal. That only deepened the bond between them. It made the intimacy safe.

One afternoon, after everybody had left the studio, they were "debriefing" in his office about the progress of the kids—whose dancing needed work, whose voice was strongest. He was reaching across his desk for some sheet music to show her when he knocked over a coffee cup.

"Fuck me," he shouted. "Fuck, fuck, fuck."

Miriam looked on, too startled to say anything.

"Oh honey," he said, "forgive the potty mouth, but my psychiatrist says if I don't say fuck at least four times a day, I'll get colitis."

He laughed, and once she started laughing, neither of them could stop. Their arms around each other, they laughed till tears were streaming down their faces.

Then he took her by the hand over to the piano; he handed her the words to what he said was his favorite song, and he had her sing it, as if she really meant it, while he played the tune. It was about a chair and how, if you wanted it, you would have to buy it, she wasn't going to give it away, since after all it had only been used once or twice and it was still nice and tight and, you see, if she couldn't sell it, she'd keep sitting on it, she wasn't gonna give it away. There was no better pair of legs in town, and no better back anywhere around, no no no—if she couldn't sell it, she was gonna sit down on it, she wasn't gonna give it away . . .

By the third refrain, they were singing together. As she

repeated, "If I can't sell it, I gonna keep sittin' on it," she wasn't anybody's wife, or anybody's mother. She was his Mae West or Marilyn Monroe; and who was he, if not her own Rock Hudson?

THEY WERE TALKING to the new student, Paul Minatelli. Blond hair, willowy frame, angelic smile, he sat between Stuart and Miriam on the piano bench, their back to the keys. His parents were divorced. He was twenty-one but looked younger. Stuart was especially taken with him; Miriam liked him, too, or tried to—one of his eyebrows seemed permanently raised above the other, which gave him an ironic, somewhat mocking air that made Miriam uncomfortable, though she did her best to hide it. He had just moved to Boston with his mother, from Asheville, North Carolina.

Stuart said, "Paul, where'd you get such adorable looks?"

Paul said, "From my father. If you think I'm cute, you should see him."

Stuart and Miriam leaned closer, smiling, as Stuart said, "Really!"

And Miriam said, "Oh do tell us more!"

Paul said, looking from Stuart to Miriam, "Not to disappoint you both, but he's married now!"

Miriam and Stuart asked, at the same time, "Happily?"

MIRIAM BREEZED IN late one evening full of excitement. She'd convinced Stuart to use one of her favorites, "Ole Buttermilk Sky," in a new review he was working up. He had also decided to let Miriam do all the choreography for the show.

At dinner, she shared the good news (she just couldn't help herself even though everyone was tired and sulky, having to wait so long for dinner). She was going on with such enthusiasm she didn't notice that Curly wasn't listening. She looked up and saw the muscles twitching in his face.

She said, "I guess I ought to quit while I'm ahead."

"And when would that be?" Curly scoffed. "What are you two, partners now? It's always "we this" and "we that"; you'd think you were running the place."

"I'm just telling you how my day was," she said. "Excuse me for thinking you'd be interested."

Curly stared at her, one finger tapping the table. "This isn't right," he said after a moment.

"What isn't right?"

"This, this job, this guy you work for, if you can call him a guy; all the time Ethan's spending practicing and performing when he ought to be doing kid things, like playing ball and hanging out. It isn't right; it isn't natural." He banged his fist down on the table. And as he stalked out, he said, "Do you even know where Julie is? When was the last time we all ate together?"

Sam started to cry. Ethan laughed at Sam.

"Now what's wrong?" she asked. "And Ethan, you can be excused. Go practice, will you?"

"My shoelaces came untied," Sam sobbed.

No, he couldn't walk in the dark down to Sigrid's house; no, she wouldn't take him. And if he wouldn't let her tie the laces, he should just shut up and do it himself. It surprised her how annoyed she was, when just a moment before she had felt elated.

Now there were two Miriams. One was back at the studio, thumbing through the *Show Boat* score, recalling all her favorite scenes and songs from that long-ago musical, already working out the dance moves for the kids. That Miriam watched her son, her youngest, the baby, from a faraway stage, and it broke her heart to see how sad and all alone he was, and if she hadn't been so far away, she would have held him in her arms. The other Miriam moved like a robotic mother, sweeping the dishes off the table and into the sink, holding them under the hard, hot jet of water while she scrubbed and scrubbed until her hands were burning, before she placed each cup and plate and bowl carefully in the rack to dry. That Miriam moved around Sam who sat at the table whimpering; that Miriam swept the floor around his feet, wiped down the Formica tabletop around his arms; she wiped and buffed and polished until the kitchen light reflected on every surface of the kitchen, glaring up at what was shining down upon it.

Scene XI

Ethan sang and danced throughout New England. He was thirteen years old when he auditioned for the road company of *The Sound of Music* and landed the part of one of the von Trapp kids. He was a little old for the part, but the casting director was so taken with him, his stage presence, his powerful voice, that he wanted to hire him anyway. Not only that, the company was willing to pay a chaperone $250 a week to look after him for the nine-month run. "That was quite a lot of money in those days," Miriam would say years later when she'd tell the story. Even Ethan was excited. He'd be away from home, he wouldn't have to go to school, and he wouldn't have his mother breathing down his neck. What was not to like? Miriam in the first dizzying moments of the spectacular news could hardly keep herself from singing "Climb Every Mountain." She called her cousins, Irene and Charlie. Everyone said, remember us when you're rich and famous.

Curly balked. Not so fast, he said. Ethan had no business being out of school and away from home for so long. He was just a kid. It was too soon. He wasn't ready. Maybe if she went on the road with him, but in that case what about Sam and Julie? Okay, Julie would soon be off to college, but Sam, Sam needed his mother, too. Besides, with the hours he was working, he couldn't do around the house what she did. They all depended on her. Maybe in a few years, but not now.

She knew he was right. She couldn't deny it. When it came to Ethan and show business, Curly was always right. There'd be other opportunities. This offer was just a sign of bigger things to come. As Stuart liked to say, the sky's the limit. Curly was right, and as he went on about what would be best for all of them, they were family, after all, a voice inside her head was singing: it had to be you, it fucking had to be you.

ETHAN WANTED TO go to his friend Finny's house for a sleepover birthday party. Because of the bed-wetting, he'd never slept over at anyone's house before and none of his friends had ever slept over at his house. He had gotten good at coming up with excuses—he had a voice lesson, he was performing out of town that night, he wasn't feeling well—but he was almost fourteen now, and he knew his friends were beginning to wonder. He wanted to give it a try. He wanted to spend the night at Finny's.

"But Ethan," Miriam said at dinner a week before the party. "Don't you think it's a little risky?"

Curly added, "Jeez, kid, imagine what happens if you have an accident."

"I won't have an accident," Ethan insisted. "I just won't sleep."

"Famous last words," Curly said. "You'd be taking a big chance."

"Darling," Miriam said, stroking his cheek, "we just don't want you to embarrass yourself."

"It'll embarrass me if I don't go. I just want to be normal for a change."

"You normal, that's a good one," Sam said.

"Quiet, Sam," Miriam said. "This is none of your business."

"What do you mean none of my business," he said. "I have a reputation, too, you know. How would it look if everybody knew my big brother wet the bed? My friends will wonder about me, if they don't already."

"Sam," Miriam barked, "not one more word."

Curly made a fist and waved it, saying, "Bang. Zoom. Straight to the moon."

"I don't care who knows," Ethan said, throwing his napkin down. "I'm sick of this whole thing. I'm sick of singing. I'm sick of Stuart. I'm sick of all of you. I want to go to this party like everybody else." He pushed away from the table and ran from the room.

Curly thought they ought to let him go. Maybe something like a sleepover with all his friends would be just the thing he needed to get over this problem. Maybe protecting him had only made it worse. Miriam was not so sure. Nothing scared her more than shame and embarrassment. She still hadn't gotten over last year's fiasco with Dr. Abdul, the tall turban-headed Brockton hypnotist who, in his ads on television, claimed to be able to cure anyone of any bad habit, or your money back. Satisfaction guaranteed. Ethan hadn't been in his office more than ten minutes when Abdul came running out to the waiting room in a rage.

"You will pay!" he said. "You will pay me now!"

"Pay you for what?" Miriam asked, standing up. "Is Ethan cured?"

"Cured?" he scoffed. "Look at him!"

Ethan stood in the doorway, yawning, a dark stain in the crotch of his chinos.

"What happened?" Miriam asked.

"I hypnotize your son, he fall asleep and wet my couch, my new couch. And now you will pay for cleaning."

"Hell I will," Miriam said. "You knew what the risk was when you put him to sleep."

"You pay for cleaning or I sue."

"So sue me!" she said. "I'm not paying one penny for the couch or the cure. Some cure. Ethan, come!"

The laughter of the other patients in the waiting room still burned in her ears.

"I don't know, Curly," she said. "I'm so afraid he'll have an accident, and you know how cruel kids can be."

"He's got to face the music sometime. Better now than later."

So they let him go. And bravely Ethan went.

And it was sometime close to four a.m. when the doorbell rang. Ethan, out of breath, sweaty, in sneakers and damp pajamas, was holding a bundle of wet sheets.

"Oh, Jesus, Ethan," Miriam said. "Did you run here? Finny lives at least a mile away."

"I tried to stay awake," he said.

"Did anybody see you leave?" Miriam asked.

"I don't think so."

"Okay," she said, "let's wash the sheets and get you cleaned up."

The sun was just coming up by the time everything was done. Miriam wanted to drive him back to Finny's but Ethan wouldn't let her. He was afraid the sound of the engine would wake the kids.

"But I can stop a block away," she said.

"No," he said. "Too risky. Better if I just run there."

"So now it's too risky?" she said.

He started to cry. "Please, Ma . . ."

"Okay," she said. "Okay. Run if you want."

Curly said. "Stop crying, kid. Some day you'll laugh about this."

As Ethan ran off carrying the sheets, Miriam said, "He should only live so long."

He came home later that morning, tired and demoralized. He said he'd gotten back without anyone waking up. He made the bed and got into it, and lay there terrified he'd fall asleep. But he'd run so fast he was drenched in sweat, and the sweat dampened the sheets through his pajamas. When the others woke and saw how wet he was, he said he must have had a fever in the night, but they of course refused to believe him, he must have wet the bed, and so they teased him after all, as if he had. He didn't want to talk about it anymore. He was too embarrassed.

Miriam hated to see him sad like this; she hated when anything bad happened to her kids. There was nothing she wouldn't do to spare them pain. And because of that, it really ticked her off that the whole sorry business could have been avoided if he'd only let her drive him back. "So maybe now you'll listen to us," she couldn't keep from saying.

"Lay off, Miriam," Curly said. "The kid feels bad enough."

That he did. That he did. If he had only listened to her.

Scene XII

Miriam and Curly were lying in bed, watching a news special on the missile crisis. The State Department spokesman was saying that under no circumstances would America permit offensive weapons to be delivered to Cuba. America demanded that the Soviets cease construction immediately and remove all warheads from Cuban soil. There was talk of a blockade and a quarantine. There were old clips of Khrushchev banging his shoe on his desk at the United Nations. There were clips of the young president in consultation with his aides at the White House. There were clips of mushroom clouds out at sea or over deserts, and experts of all kinds describing in graphic detail which cities would be targeted and what the short- and long-term effects of such a holocaust would be. The doomsday clock would soon be moved closer to midnight, if it wasn't there already.

Miriam couldn't bear to watch. She looked at her night table to the right of the television. She looked at the photograph of

Miss Julie from *Show Boat* above the night table mirror, and in the mirror she could see the *South Pacific* poster on the wall above her bed. And there beside the mirror was her red jewelry box inside of which were some of Bubbie's old bracelets, a diamond engagement ring that belonged to Bubbie's mother, which Bubbie had given Miriam when she and Curly had gotten engaged, which Miriam would give to Julie when the right man came along. And there were rings inside the box and pendants that signified some special place or person from her past. There was even a brooch among them that Frankie Kaufman had given her on the occasion of their one-month anniversary of going steady. She looked at her neatly arranged cosmetics—the eyeliner case, the jar of vanishing cream, the little tubes of lipstick—the pictures of her children on the chest of drawers beside the table. She looked at her open, walk-in closet to the left of the bedroom door—the boxes of shoes stacked on the floor beneath the two rows of hanging blouses, sweaters, dresses for any season, some in the far back from her mother's old shop, some dating back to high school. Oh, she could tell you which store each dress, each outfit came from, and which ones were gifts, from whom, and on what occasions, so many of them gifts from Curly for her birthday or anniversary, many of them gifts he bought her after some fight or argument as a way of saying sorry, making up. Each one was a reminder, so it seemed just then, of how much he loved her, of how much she meant to him. What was the bedroom, or the house itself, but the story of her life, their life, their day-to-day existence, rooted in a history, for good or ill, unique to her and to her family, defining them all, keeping them all safely who they were—until tonight. Tonight, that history offered no more safety than a piece of tissue, a scrap of gossamer, a dustball to be vaporized to nothing in the first flash of the horrible bomb.

She could hear footsteps overhead and a door close, she could hear water running, the children upstairs getting ready for bed, in the middle of their nightly rituals. There was great comfort in the sound. And there always had been. Some nights, when all the lights were out, she'd sneak upstairs to check on the children, to listen to the slow and steady rhythm of their breathing as they slept. Sometimes she'd hear the boys whispering to each other, giggling over who knew what. Sometimes she'd hear Ethan singing a lullaby softly to himself or to Sam in the darkness. He'd be singing one of the lullabies she used to sing to them when they were little. Why didn't she still do that? Why the hurry to grow up? Wasn't it her job to keep them all safe, to help them think, as long as possible, that their lives would just go on like this forever, that nothing could imperil the world they made together?

She realized that she had taken Curly's hand, or had he taken hers, as aerial photographs of Cuba flashed across the screen. She squeezed it tighter as if to keep herself, the house, and everyone she loved from vanishing before her very eyes.

One night at bedtime a few weeks later, she found Sam sitting on the porch. It was a chilly clear November night.

In only pajamas and slippers, Sam was sitting on the edge of a lounge chair, looking up at the sky.

"Sam," she said, "what in the world are you doing out here? You want to make yourself sick?"

"Ma," he said, "do you feel the earth move?"

"Earth move?" she asked, "like when you fall in love?"

"What, are you nuts?" he said. "No, like just move, like around the sun."

"No, of course not," she said, laughing. "You can't feel that."

"Yeah," he said, and shivered. "Gravity, right? That's what Mr. Pincus told us today in Hebrew school. We're spinning at something like forty thousand miles per hour, but we don't feel a thing because of gravity."

She sat down and put her arm around him.

"But what the heck is gravity?" he continued.

"It's what holds us to the ground," she said. "But we need to go inside now, honey. You're shivering."

"Yeah, yeah, okay, in a second, but, Ma, listen, how could we be moving that fast and not know it. I mean that's faster than the fastest roller coaster. Why aren't we screaming?"

"Why is Mr. Pincus talking about gravity in Hebrew school?"

"I don't know," Sam said. "We were talking about Adam and Eve and the apple, and he just started talking about outer space."

"But what does outer space have to do with anything?"

"He just looked really sad," Sam said. "Well, not sad exactly, or just sad, but also angry too."

"Angry?" Miriam asked. "At who?"

"God," Sam said. "He said he didn't understand what God had in mind with all the suffering he brings us, all the wars and nuclear bombs and death camps. Or why he'd put us in an empty universe surrounded by a vacuum."

"He shouldn't be talking to you kids about stuff like that."

"And you know what?" Sam asked.

"What?"

"He said you were angry, too."

"Me? What you do mean, me? I've never said two words to Mr. Pincus."

"He said everyone your age is angry and if you weren't angry, you were stupid."

"Well," Miriam said, "I'm not stupid, am I?"

"No," Sam said, yawning, "but you get angry a lot. At Ethan when he doesn't practice. At Julie when she doesn't listen. At me when I wet the bed or cry or ask too many questions."

"Well, um, sometimes, maybe," she stammered. "Not a lot. And anyway it's different."

"Why?" Sam asked.

"I'm just busy, Sam, I'm not really angry." And as she said this, she did get angry. She wanted to justify herself, to explain herself. She wanted Sam and everyone, even Curly, even her mother, to understand her, to know how much she loved them, how much she wanted only what was best for them, but it was really hard sometimes, more often than she cared to think, not to get frustrated, especially given how short life was. And, yes, how much suffering there was everywhere. She wasn't stupid. She knew how bad things could be.

She hugged Sam, who by then was leaning against her. She said, "Darling, don't forget how much I love you. If I lose my temper, it's only cause I want you—I want everyone—to be happy. It's so important to be happy."

"Like in the song?" he asked.

"What song?"

" 'Put on a Happy Face.' "

"Yeah, darling, just like in the song."

"Okay, Ma," he said as he yawned again. "But who the heck is Mrs. Murphy?"

"Mrs. Murphy?" she asked. She really had to get this child to bed.

"The lady in the psalm," he said. "You know, Mrs Murphy. Mr. Pincus was talking about her today, too. How in such a crazy world she's all we really have."

"What psalm?"

"The twenty-third one," he said, yawning and stretching.

"There's no Mrs. Murphy in the twenty-third psalm, or any other psalm. What in the world is Mr. Pincus teaching you kids?"

"Yeah, sure there is, Ma," he said, half asleep. "You know where it says, 'Good Mrs. Murphy shall follow me all the days of my life.' "

"Oh Sam, sweetheart," she laughed, "it isn't 'Good Mrs.

Murphy,' it's 'goodness and mercy': 'goodness and mercy shall follow me all the days of my life.' "

But Sam was gone by then. She gathered him up in her arms and carried him to bed. She tucked him in as snugly as she could, and lay down next to him and prayed, "Please, God, keep away from my children. You hear me? Keep away."

Scene XIII

Miriam didn't trust this Paul kid, not one bit. Oh, he was talented, sure, but there was something about him (she couldn't put her finger on it) that was up to no good, something underhanded, shady. That eyebrow of his seemed to rise mockingly whenever he looked at her. He'd smile at her but not with any warmth; he smiled too quickly, as if to cover up a scowl or a sneer. Yes, he could really belt out a tune, and with his long frame he tap danced like a young Gene Kelly. Ethan was shorter and stockier, and while his dance technique was flawless, even Miriam could see that he lacked a certain flair or freedom that Paul possessed. Ethan admired Paul. In fact, he seemed to worship him. And Paul played him like a fiddle. In rehearsal, when Stuart wasn't looking, he'd poke Ethan or say something under his breath that made Ethan laugh, lose his concentration, and forget his steps, while Paul, the little angel, smiling innocently, sailed through the routine. "Ethan," Stuart would yell, "pay attention, would you—just do it like Paul, for once!" Couldn't Stuart see that Paul was egging Ethan on? When she'd try to tell him, he would pat her on the back and say, "Now, now, stage mom, a little jealous?"

HER STEPMOTHER CALLED to tell her that her father had "passed away in his sleep." She had anticipated this moment her whole life, it seemed—rehearsed it, mourned it in advance, composed and recomposed the obituary that described a kind and devoted father, a father who lived for nothing but his only daughter and his grandchildren, a father whom his daughter and grandchildren would never replace or forget. She had imagined the grief, the fits of sobbing, Curly and the children gathering round her to console her, to console each other, the condolence cards and letters she'd receive from friends of his, who'd want her to know what a wonderful man he had been and how very much he had loved her. But when she heard the words "passed away in his sleep," it was like she was a little girl again, facing him in the doorway of the old apartment—watching him fumble with some poorly wrapped trinket that he would hand her and then hurry off back into the life she knew next to nothing about. A butcher in the same shop for nearly fifty years, who married the wrong woman when she was just a girl, a child really—and then married the right one, a woman as quiet as he was, as unassuming and nondescript, and together they lived happily or unhappily or, for all she knew, anywhere in between. You could say that for sixty-five years he had passed away in a bed in a small apartment, and now for all eternity he'd pass away in a box in the ground. What surprised her now, as she thought this, was the grief she didn't feel. She was crying now for the absence of that grief. She was mourning everything between her and her father that had never taken place.

THEN A FEW months later Bubbie died. The president was assassinated. Camelot was gone. And not long after that, her mother took a serious fall and broke her arm. It was clear to everyone she couldn't do for herself any longer. But who would take her in? Miriam asked her cousins Charlie and Irene, but they declined. What with this and that going on, they couldn't do it, much as they'd like to; maybe in a year or so, when things ease up, but not now, no, they couldn't, it wouldn't be fair to their kids. Besides, they said, your mother's loaded; she can afford a nursing home. But Miriam wouldn't dump her mother in a nursing home. Not in this lifetime. In that case, then, they said, being her daughter, you should take her in.

What could she do? She and Curly were barely getting by, even with both of them working; they had no time for the kids, or for each other (not that having time in that department would have made much difference). And despite her mother's wealth—whatever wealth there was, no one really knew—Miriam was certain she herself would never see a penny of it. Tula would just be one more mouth to feed. And what about the kids, what would it be like for them to have to live with such an old, sick woman, and where would she put her?

What did she owe her mother anyway? She had had a tough life, sure. But she was hardly a mother, really. She had made a lot of money and had once taken Miriam to New York to see a show. But mostly she had never been around, off living her "real" life with Mr. Perez. And even when she had been around, she had seldom been available. Maybe Tula had had her reasons. But the fact is, she had left her only daughter for other people to raise. Her mother pretty much had done whatever the hell she had wanted to do. Miriam was the last thing she had ever thought of. Really, when it came right down to it, her mother had never known the first thing about being a mother. But Miriam, her daughter, she had learned the hard way what it meant to be a mother. She knew the meaning of sacrifice, devotion, and loyalty. She knew what a mother was supposed to do, and now, once again, it was up to her to do it. And she would do it. How could she not? She'd show her mother what a mother was.

HER MOTHER MOVED in, and it seemed to Miriam that everyone retreated from one another. Sam, of course was Sam, off in his own little world. But now Ethan, too, like Julie, was hardly ever at home. When he wasn't performing, Ethan was out with friends. Julie had gotten into Antioch on a full academic scholarship and would be leaving in the fall, but really it felt to Miriam as if she had already left. At dinner, both kids would wolf down their food and bolt. Her mother's obesity and incontinence disgusted them; it embarrassed them to bring friends to the house, because she was always there, always complaining, always demanding this or that, or wishing she was dead already. Miriam couldn't blame them, but out of respect for her, couldn't they treat her mother with a little kindness, if only to make *her* life easier, so her mother wouldn't be at her as she always was whenever she got home from work? They'd roll their eyes at all her pleading and disappear into their lives.

"Can't you see what's happening?" Curly asked one night, as he was getting into bed.

"So what am I supposed to do?" she responded, laying her book down on her chest.

"Put her in a nursing home, for starters," Curly said.

Across the room in the mirror above her dressing table, she saw herself, her face, beneath the *South Pacific* poster—just over her head, Emile de Becque was singing as he held Nellie Forbush at sunset under a palm tree on a Polynesian beach—the vibrant reds and blues, the incandescent whiteness of the sand made Miriam's face seem paler by comparison; her face looked ghostly, she could almost see right through it.

"Miriam, are you listening to me?"

"What?"

"A nursing home—we should put your mother in a nursing home."

"You'd like that, wouldn't you?"

"That's not the point," he said. "She'd be safe there. There'd be people, professionals, to take care of her. She might even make friends."

"Would you dump your father in a nursing home?"

"Look what she's doing to the kids," he said. "They can't stand to be around her."

What song was Emile singing? "Some Enchanted Evening"?

"Miriam," he shouted.

"What?"

"We can't do this, I can't do this. Tula won't give us a penny to help out. You got your girl Melba coming twice a week now, which we can't afford. And for what? I'm telling you, I work too goddamn hard to come home to her, to this. This is tearing us apart. The kids are suffering."

"You never answered my question," she said.

"What question?"

"About your father—what you would do if it was your father we were talking about."

"Well, it isn't," he said. "And my father hasn't had a stroke and doesn't shit and piss everywhere but in the hopper."

"So we'll move out, okay, my mother and me. Will that make you happy?"

"No comment," he muttered.

"What?"

"Nothing," he said. "Never mind. Forget it."

He turned out his light and she turned out hers.

Some evening, she thought. Some enchanted evening.

HER MOTHER HAD called Miriam just as she was leaving the studio to tell her to pick up mouthwash and dietary candy on her way home. She also had to pick up dinner, and Curly's dress suit at the dry cleaner, and she was running late as it was. But what the hell could she do. Only later, as she was leaving the pharmacy did she realize that she had left her Gershwin songbook in the studio. She was supposed to find a number that Ethan might use in his callback for a summer stock production of *Funny Face.*

The studio was locked and dark. The darkness and the quiet soothed her as she climbed the stairs to the office. She would just sit here for a minute. It was already way too late to forestall the bickering in store for her when she got home. "Party girl," her mother would call her; Curly would start with her, too, about the little "faygela," and the kids, the kids would be at one another's throats by now. She couldn't stand it anymore. She wanted to just sit there for a little while. She wanted to think about songs for Ethan without Ethan and his temper tantrums getting in the way; she wanted to sit there, as she was doing now, in the dark office, with the desk piled high with songbooks, with the shadowy studio through the window in front of her, here where there was no one to feed or fend off, no one to fight with, or appease.

The phone rang and she woke. How long had she been sleeping?

"Where the hell are you," Curly was shouting.

"I was just, um . . ."

"You were just what? Why are you still there? What are you two doing? You've got a family, for Christ's sake!"

Staring straight ahead, she held the phone out from her ear; Curly's voice was a far-off insect buzzing. She wasn't listening; she was watching something moving in the studio, a shadow by the piano, no, two shadows, one taller than the other, and thinner, too, both bending over, moving, picking things up, putting things on, dressing, as they hurried out. She could hear the footsteps running down the stairs—was that Stuart laughing?—and the door slam.

Did she dream this? Was she dreaming now? She could still hear Curly's tiny shouting as she hung up the phone. Dream or no dream, whatever it was, it was not to be looked at, not to be thought of. That much she knew. And the sensations that came and went almost too swiftly to be felt—shame, fear, revulsion, humiliation, excitement (why did she feel shame? what had she done wrong?)—what were they but the disintegrating traces of a bad dream from which she would eventually wake up?

To steady her breathing, she tried to think of nothing. As if nothing had happened, as if pretending as much would make it so, she walked slowly out of the office and down the stairs. For the second time that night, she left without the Gershwin songbook, though this time she wouldn't remember what it was she had forgotten, what it was she'd come back to the studio to get.

THE NEXT DAY she did not show up for work. When she didn't show up the day after that, Stuart called.

"Miriam, my pet," he said, as spritely as ever, "are we under the weather?"

She couldn't think of what to say. She put out her cigarette and placed her free hand on the kitchen table to keep herself from trembling.

"Miriam? Are you there?"

"Stuart, listen," she finally said.

"I'm all ears," he said.

"I was at the studio two nights ago."

"What a coincidence," he said. "So was I."

When she didn't say anything, he added, "Miriam, what did you expect? What do you think I do for kicks, go home each night and listen to 'There Is Nothing Like a Dame'? What do you think, I just pretend with you all day?"

"I didn't think that, at the studio . . ."

"That what? That I'd 'use' the studio? Desecrate the inner sanctum?"

"But what would people say?"

"What people?" he said. "No one else was there."

"I was," she said.

"Yeah, you were, and what are you going to do, break it to the press?"

"But someone could," she said, her voice quavering, "and then what?"

"Then this," he said.

"What?"

"Just this. The two of us talking."

"There'd be more than just the two of us talking, you know that. Think of the scandal. The repercussions."

"Come on," he said. "We're grown-ups, aren't we? You pays your money, you takes your chances."

"I can't," she said. "I have a family to think of."

"Maybe you do, dear," he said. "But let's be honest. It isn't 'the family' you're thinking of."

Miriam was silent.

"Sweetie," he continued, "tell yourself whatever story you need to tell—but don't give me a song and dance about your family. I'm a fag. I'm not an idiot."

"I wish you wouldn't use that word," she said.

"How about I call myself a man's man, a regular guy, one of the boys? Curly would approve of that, wouldn't he?"

"Was that Paul with you?"

"What difference does it make, stage mom? Should I have been with Ethan?"

"How could you say such a thing? How could you do such a thing? I thought, I thought . . ."

"Your problem, Miriam, is you don't think. You dream. Everything you love's a dream."

"The sooner I wake up from this one, the better." She slammed the phone down.

Her mother was standing in the kitchen doorway watching her. "Who was that?" she asked. "What's wrong? Why were you yelling?"

"Nothing's wrong," she said. "I'm fine. Everything's fine."

"Lucky you," her mother said. "A regular Madame Butterfly."

When anyone would ask her why she had quit her job, she'd tell them what she told herself (as if pretending it were so could make it so): that Ethan would be moving to New York soon, and since there wasn't much more Stuart could do for him, there was no real reason for her to stay on. She could make more money doing something else. Then she'd shrug and change the subject. She couldn't imagine telling anyone the truth, certainly not Curly, or any of her friends. She wouldn't know where to start, or what to say, what language to use. In every imagined telling of the story—"I saw two 'confirmed bachelors' committing sodomy," "I saw two homosexuals having intercourse," "I saw this naked faygela I used to worship fucking another faygela, his student, up the ass"—she didn't recognize herself. It was like someone had changed scripts on her in the middle of a scene, and so it wasn't that she couldn't remember what her lines were, but that there were no lines, none anyway that she'd been trained to say.

She wanted Curly to touch her only when they were in public, and not because she wanted everyone to think they were a happily married couple but simply because she couldn't stand the thought of being talked about. She wanted him to hold her hand when they were out with friends, or put his arm around her or even kiss her on the cheek in front of others, so they would think her marriage was the same as theirs. That way, other people, what they said or how they saw her, wouldn't matter. She was tired of other people mattering. Creating the impression that there was nothing wrong was how she kept the world from entering her mind.

Home, however, meant being left alone, home was where she had no reason to be touched, because she didn't have to care about what anybody thought.

The night before, after everyone had gone to sleep, he slipped into her bed. Oh, she did feel sorry for him. She knew how unhappy he was, how much he craved the physical attention she was incapable of giving, especially now. He deserved a wife for whom intimacy wasn't such a fearful chaos, a wife who was able to love him in all the ways he needed, who didn't lie there like a mannequin in bed. She wasn't the "cold bitch" she imagined he imagined her to be. She understood his need for consolation if not relief. The falling-out with his brother over money, and his new job at Lord & Taylor which paid even less than she was making, temping as a secretary at a nearby college—all of this drew him to her bed more frequently these days, for all the things she couldn't find it in herself to give. Whatever he might have thought, she got no pleasure from his disappointment.

He said, "Sweetheart, it's been so long, couldn't we, tonight?"

"I can't, Curly," she said. "Please, forgive me, but I just can't."

"Why not? What did I do? We're married, aren't we?" His hand rested on her shoulder, heavy as a mallet. She slid out from under it.

"It's just too late for that," she said.

"Too late, as in tonight," he asked, "or too late, as in for good?"

"Tonight," she said, "but . . ."

"But what?"

"I don't know, maybe; I just feel it's just all such a mess. I don't know what to do. I'm sorry."

"So what are you saying?" he asked. "You want a divorce?"

"No, not that. The kids, my mother. The family. We are a family. No, I don't want that."

"Then what?" Now he was leaning over her. "What about me? What am I supposed to do?"

"I have no idea," she said. "I'm sorry, but I don't know."

She wanted to tell him that she loved him, and that—that what? That he deserved to be happy, that she'd always tried to make him happy? That she had never thought, never dreamed that marriage—not just theirs but any marriage—could be like this, like being trapped inside a scene that just won't end the way she wanted it to although, just then, if he asked her what it was she really wanted she could not have said?

"I just thought with Stuart out of the picture . . ."

"Stuart has nothing to do with this." She turned away and pulled the covers up over her shoulder.

He threw the sheet off roughly and left the room, slamming the door behind him.

She lay awake for hours trying to make sense of what had happened—but she couldn't make sense of it. She couldn't make sense of herself, of anything. All night she lay there thinking, nonsensically, that Stuart was out of the picture because he wasn't; that he wasn't out of the picture because he was.

Scene XIV

From the end of the hall, Sam could hear the whir of shuffled cards, and then the slap, slap, slap on the Formica table. As he came down the dark hall, he could see through the kitchen doorway, in the lamplight, her hands turning over card after card. He had wet the bed again and come downstairs to find her. Everyone else in the house was sleeping. His grandmother snored and murmured from what used to be the upstairs playroom, the room next to the bedroom that he and his brother shared. To get downstairs, he had had to leap over the nightly puddle of pee she left outside his room, the little accidents she had because she couldn't move fast enough to make it to the toilet. Between his grandmother and him, his mother often said, the house smelled like a flophouse, like a sewer. His mother wouldn't be happy to see him. She would say, what am I gonna do with you? When are you gonna grow up? Don't I have enough to do already?

Anger shrank the house. You couldn't turn around without

getting yelled at. She and his father fought about her mother. She and her mother fought about hairspray or brands of coffee, or whatever it was his mother was supposed to get for Tula and didn't or got wrong. She and Ethan fought about his voice, his practicing. Julie was never around anymore to fight with, which was what her parents fought with her about when she was around. Sam tried to stay out of everybody's way. But the house was shrinking. During the day, the only hiding place that remained was good behavior. He had stopped caring about his shirt and shoelaces. Even though his throat hurt when he cut his food, he cut his food. He was quieter now. He didn't ask so many questions. He tried to do what he was told and not get in anybody's way, but every night the wet bed dragged him out of hiding. He said, "Ma, I need you." She stared down at the cards her hands were flipping over and moving from column to column; it was as if her hands were independent of her body, moving by themselves. Next to the cards, there was a cup of coffee; next to the coffee, an ashtray with a cigarette leaning against the grooved lip. Little curls of smoke were rising from it. "Go back to bed," she said in a flat voice, not even looking up. It was just a body, not his mother speaking. Where she had gone, he had no idea. "Go back to bed before I scream."

From that night on, he no longer left his bedroom when he wet the bed. He'd strip the sheets off and slip free of the damp pajamas. He'd find a thin edge of mattress that wasn't wet and lie along it on his side, trying not to move as he fell asleep with the house shrinking all around him.

Unable to sleep, she'd sit at the kitchen table playing solitaire for hours, slapping the cards down on the Formica table, sliding the cards from one column to another, watching and not watching as the columns grew and shrank, and shrank and grew, while the cigarette she never lifted burned down to nothing in the ashtray, and the coffee cooled. And as she played game after game long into the night, shifting the cards by suit or sequence, the royal families broken apart and struggling (by her hand alone) to reunite, fragments of memories flashed randomly before her from the near and distant past: there was Stuart at the piano, singing as he played, his face at once exuberant with pleasure and somehow menacing, bright lit and shadowy, giving way to Curly's face, his handsome, loving face, the face he watched her with the night they met, becoming suddenly his needy face, his disappointed face, one moment sorrowful, the next enraged, changing, in turn, into her mother's face reflected in the window of a train, young, beautiful, so charming to the world, so harsh to her only daughter. And there was Sam's face crying, or Ethan's pitching a fit because he didn't want to practice, or Julie's staring at her with that blank, infuriating, you-can't-do-anything-for-me expression that Miriam couldn't help but hate, and hate herself for hating. Only God knew how much she loved them. Only God knew how terrible the world could be, how vulnerable the children were, and what it took to get them ready for the trials that surely lay ahead. Only God knew she never meant to hurt them, and when she did hurt them sometimes (she wasn't perfect, who was?), when she spoke too brusquely, when she shook them harder than she meant to, or ignored them, or responded coldly or impatiently to pleas for help, to pleas (oh God) for love, yes, only God knew how much she suffered when they suffered, how indelibly into her heart their pain was stamped.

Long into the night she watched the broken royal families drift from column onto column, searching for the proper suit and sequence over the kitchen table between the untouched cigarette burning in the ashtray and the coffee cooling in the cup.

At eleven years old, Sam was the only one left to look after his grandmother. Miriam hated to demand this of him, he was too young for this kind of thing. It wasn't right to ask a child to do this, she knew that, she felt terrible about it, but what choice did she have? They couldn't afford to have Melba come once a week. Even if she, Miriam, wanted to, she couldn't afford to quit her new job as a secretary at Happy Trails, a local travel agency, not now, not with Curly making peanuts. She just couldn't continue running her mother's errands after work each day—medication, mouthwash, dietary candy, cigarettes—and nothing in her mother's eyes was right or ever enough, she couldn't do anything right, and lately she hadn't been getting home till seven. She'd apologize for getting home so late, and her mother would scoff—party girl, you, you're just a party girl, you never think of anybody but yourself. And tired as she was, there'd be an angry pool of urine waiting for her to wipe up on the kitchen floor or outside the bathroom her mother hadn't reached in time.

Ethan and Julie were already well launched into their lives. There was just no other way around it. Sam would have to run home between elementary school and Hebrew school and check on his grandmother, make sure she was all right, and didn't need anything.

What surprised her was how he took the news. Okay, Ma, he said, okay, but not like he was trying to be helpful, or not only that; but like he knew his not whining or complaining would disturb her more than if he pitched a fit.

Without a fuss, he ran home after school. He cleaned up after his grandmother. He'd go to stores and get her whatever she needed or wanted.

Then one night, a school night, and after his bedtime, she caught him leaving the house.

"Where do you think you're going?"

"Grandma needs cigarettes, and saccharin, and she said, while I'm at it, I should get us a couple of sundaes at Brigham's."

"On a school night, after bedtime? I don't think so."

"I don't know," he said, looking down at his feet. "She'll be real disappointed, Ma."

"I don't care what she is," she said. "It's too late for you to be running all over town for her."

Her mother called down from upstairs, "Let the boy go, goddamn it; I need cigarettes and you're too busy, miss party girl, to get them."

"Mother," Miriam called back, "it's too late, he has school tomorrow, and he's just a boy!"

"And you're just a party girl!" Now her mother was crying. "Oy Gott, I should just be dead already. What did I do to deserve such a daughter?"

They could hear her huffing and puffing as she shuffled back into her room.

"Jesus, okay," Miriam said, "go get her whatever the hell she wants. But only tonight. Never again."

But from then on her mother sent him out most every night. And not only that, when he'd return they would stay up late watching TV and talking, with the door shut. Sometimes, Miriam would creep up the stairs and put her ear to the door, though she couldn't make out what it was they said. Sometimes she thought he was performing for her, telling her jokes, doing impressions, maybe imitating the comics they'd seen on the Johnny Carson show. She could hear her mother laughing. It was the only time she ever heard her mother laugh. What did they talk about? Sam would never say, and her mother would only smile, as if to say, such a good boy, and so talented.

Sam wasn't getting the sleep he needed; what with the late-night television and the bedwetting, he'd be especially cranky in the mornings. And the Hebrew school had called to say that he was failing and in danger of being kept back. But what could she do? She and Curly were just too tired at night to police them. They demanded that the late nights stop and then pretended that they had. He *was* a good boy, Miriam told herself. There was no denying that. She should feel grateful. But there was something in the way he was being good that she didn't like; something about it, she couldn't say what, didn't feel good at all.

THEN SAM STARTED telling jokes, one-liners—Henny Youngman, Rodney Dangerfield, Myron Cohen, Milton Berle. He must have been getting the jokes from all the late-night television in her mother's room. Lately, at dinner, particularly when nothing was being said, or when the bickering started, he would say them one after another in rapid fire:

"Went to a child psychiatrist the other day; the kid didn't do a thing for me.

"Went to a psychiatrist, he said what do you do? I said I'm a mechanic, he said good you get under the couch.

"I was so ugly when I was born my mother had to breast-feed me through a straw.

"My mother refused to breast-feed me. She said she just wanted to be friends.

"She told the lifeguard at the pool to keep an eye off me.

"My proctologist stuck his finger in my mouth.

"My wife and I bumped into her old boyfriend, Bob. 'Bob,' she said, 'this is Sam. Sam this is good-bye.'

"When I got home from work, my wife met me at the door dressed in nothing but Saran Wrap. What, I said, leftovers again?

"She says to me what would it take to get you to go on a second honeymoon? And I say, A second wife.

"She says, why don't you take me somewhere I've never been before? I say, how 'bout the kitchen?"

There was something manic in the joke-telling, as if he thought that if he didn't tell them all as fast as possible something horrible would happen. She wondered if his quirkiness was finally turning into real insanity. For a moment she pictured him in the nuthouse, doing stand-up in a padded cell.

Only her mother would laugh at the jokes. The two of them—it was like they were in league together, up to no good somehow at her expense, but she couldn't say exactly how or why.

"If it weren't for pickpockets, I'd have no sex at all.

"At my age eating's more fun than sex; I've put a mirror over the dinner table."

After a while Miriam would say, "Enough already. Let us eat in peace."

Her mother would still be laughing. Her mother would say, "Take my daughter!" And Sam would reply on cue, "Please."

Scene XV

They were driving to Julie's high school graduation: Curly behind the wheel, Tula beside him, and Miriam and Sam in the backseat. Julie and Ethan were already at the high school. They had just started down Webster, a narrow one-way street, when someone trying to pass them, horn blaring, drove them right up onto the sidewalk. Curly honked back long and hard, and the other car screeched to a halt. The door flew open; the man jumped out and ran toward them. He was extremely tall, heavyset, and he staggered a little as he ran. "Oh great," Curly said, "a fucking lush." Then he told them all to stay put and lock the door behind him. Miriam's mother kept repeating, "Oy Gott, oy Gott." Next thing they knew Curly and the man were shouting; what was said, they couldn't tell, because now the windows were rolled up and the doors locked. All at once, Curly swung and hit the guy square in the face, and the guy collapsed. Curly jumped back into the car and they hurried off.

By the time they turned the corner onto Park Street, the man had gotten to his knees and was touching his nose and cheek, feeling for damage. Blood ran from Curly's knuckles, down the back of his hand, staining the starched cuff of his shirt and dripping onto his tan slacks.

Miriam had seen flashes of his anger. She had always sensed the possibility of violence just under the surface of their testy day-to-day relations; she felt it, too, when he'd lose his temper at the kids over a forgotten chore, a not adequately respectful tone of voice, or any kind of trouble they got into. She felt it in the way he'd roughhouse with the boys, hurting them sometimes inadvertently. Sometimes he'd pretend to lose control so convincingly that she thought he had. Most of all, she'd felt and feared it on those nights (which now thank God rarely happened—she could thank Stuart for that) when she would turn away from him in bed, when he would throw the covers off and leave the room, or worse just lie there brooding, saying nothing.

Curly kept repeating, "Son of a bitch. Goddamn son of a bitch." He told Sam that all he was doing was protecting himself, protecting his family. He hit first because the schmuck was drunk and twice his size and he wasn't going to give him any advantage. Better not to fight than fight, he said. Walk away if you can. But if you can't, always throw the first punch.

Sam leaned over, one hand on Curly's shoulder. He was staring amazed at the bloody knuckles. He said, "Drunk stops a man on the sidewalk. Says, buddy, can you tell me where the other side of the street is? and the man says, over there. The drunk says, I was over there and someone told me it was over here."

"Enough, Sam," Miriam said. "Leave your father alone."

They drove the rest of the way in silence. Curly kept flexing his bloody hand, cursing under his breath; the boy stared out the window; Miriam found it hard to breathe, her heart was racing; the incident had come and gone in a moment, and the day now looked as peaceful as it had just minutes ago, but she couldn't let it go, that violence; its aftershock went on inside her. The roughhousing at home, the stifled angers, the frustrations, everyone in the family so often, too often, in each other's way, who knew why, or what to do about it, and every moment it was getting worse.

THIS WAS 1964. The speaker at the graduation, a local politician, spoke about the dangers Julie and her classmates would be facing in the years to come: the doomsday clock, the power of the Soviet Union, the rise of communist regimes around the world. He said that we're a peaceful country; we are slow to anger, but once provoked we would crush the enemies of freedom with an irresistible force. Sooner or later, he said, each and every one of us will be called on to defend our way of life. We were heading into a time of national sacrifice. The more he spoke, the more Miriam could feel the world around her growing large with rage, and the more it grew, the smaller she and her children seemed inside it. They were small and growing smaller. At any moment, they might disappear.

It was Julie's first night home from Antioch during fall break. She was out with friends, and Miriam was straightening up her room when she came across her diary, the gold lamé one Miriam had given her as a high school graduation present. It was unlocked and open on her desk. Miriam knew she shouldn't, but she couldn't help herself. She'd always wondered what college life was like and she could get no details from Julie who brushed her off with "It's just college, Ma, nothing to write home about." Just college! Who knew what opportunities Miriam would have had, what kind of life she might have led, had she been able to go to college? She'd have married someone like Frankie, someone with ambition and talent. Why, she might have become a professor herself. A professor of theater!

Julie had no interest in theater. Maybe that's why their relationship was always bristly and tense, why Julie had always been so unavailable. Julie's subjects were sociology, political science, and history, subjects Miriam found depressing. Where was the music in that? It didn't surprise her to see words like "injustice," "cold war," "communist," and "communism" reappearing on the pages she was scanning; but words like "pigs" and "honkies," "sit-in" and "rally" made her slow down and read more carefully. Julie had joined the Communist Party. Julie had become a radical activist against the war. If the administration didn't change course soon, she and her cohorts would take more drastic measures. Julie's boyfriend (Julie's boyfriend?) was black. They were living together. They were "fucking"—that's the word Julie used, "fucking!" which she described in disgusting detail. And then Miriam came across a passage about her and Curly—Julie couldn't wait to tell "them" the truth, so they would see her for the person she is, not the girl of their fantasies. Their whole little racist world was based in fantasy. Her mother's especially. She couldn't wait to see the look on their faces when she told them the truth.

Who was this child? Had she always thought this way? Had she always believed these horrible things? Was this, this anger and contempt for everything her parents represented what lay behind her often blank expression, her remoteness, her "independence"? Why hadn't she and Curly ever seen or guessed what had to have been stirring all these years inside their daughter? They were close, Miriam and Julie, weren't they? Hadn't she given Julie all the mothering that her own mother withheld from her?

And now what? Should she show the diary to Curly? Oh God, to think what he might do. Maybe she could talk to Julie herself; maybe mother to daughter she could get through to her, show her how this was just a phase, that she was ruining her life. But when she tried to imagine talking with Julie about such intimate things, such sensitive things, she couldn't picture it. She wasn't a racist, no, but that didn't mean she had to give her blessing to her daughter's . . . no, she couldn't do it. She couldn't do it by herself. She and Curly both would have to sit her down. They were still a family. They'd have to work this out together.

"Curly," she called downstairs, "Curly, come up here. You need to see this."

CURLY WAS HOLDING the diary when Julie got home.

"Shacking up with schvartzas?" he shouted. "Overthrowing the government? Is that what we sent you to college for?"

"You had no right to read my diary," Julie said.

"No right?" Miriam said, "We're your parents."

"Well, you don't own me. I can do what I want."

"Not in this house," Curly said. "Not as long as you're under my roof."

"How could you do this to us?" Miriam asked.

"I'm not doing anything to you. I'm living my life."

"And what we think," Miriam sobbed, "what we care about, what other people think, that doesn't matter to you, does it?"

Julie lunged for the diary and Curly pushed her back. He raised his hand to hit her, but Miriam caught it. "Curly," she cried, "don't hit her. Don't you dare hit my daughter."

She threw herself against him to hold him back.

"I'm not your daughter," Julie said.

"You're damn right, you're not," Curly shouted. "Get your things, get out. Go back to your schvartzas. You're no child of ours."

Julie ran up to her room, up the stairs past Miriam's mother who was coming down.

"Oy Gottenyu," she said. "You spoiled that girl, you ruined her. It serves you right."

Miriam looked at her mother, just looked at her, her eyes bright with hatred. "Look what you've done to me! Are you happy now, you bitch, you fucking bitch?"—that was what Miriam wanted to say, but did not. Without a word, Miriam ran into her bedroom, slamming the door behind her.

The old woman hobbled back upstairs, panting, saying "Oy Gottenyu, oy Gottenyu."

And it was over, staged like a scene in a musical, a tragic musical about abandonment, betrayal, revenge, though without the score, without the singing and dancing.

BEHIND CURLY'S BACK, Miriam wrote Julie every week. At first she wrote long letters about the importance of parental respect and how she and Curly had lived a lot longer than Julie and knew a thing or two about the world and how to live in it. Experience ought to count for something. And her experience had shown her in no uncertain terms that the world today just isn't ready for interracial romance. It may not be right, it may not be fair; in a perfect world, we'd all be colorblind. But the world is anything but perfect, and you have to live in this world, not a dream world of commendable ideals, if you want to get ahead. Julie never wrote back. And Miriam's letters got shorter. She told Julie she loved her and only wanted what was best for her. She said you may think your friends can substitute for family, but only your family would be there for you in a pinch. Eventually, all she sent were cards with news of Ethan and where he was performing and the reviews he had received. She never stopped believing, not for a second, that her daughter, her only daughter whom she missed so much, would come around to her way of thinking. Julie just needed to grow up a little bit, to learn a little more about life.

Maybe her mistake was to name her Julie in the first place. Maybe the name fated her to this, who knew? So maybe now she should think of her as Chava, the wayward daughter in the new hit musical *Fiddler on the Roof,* her banished waif; maybe that would make the heartbreak somehow less unbearable, at least while she listened to the songs or sang them to herself—for a little while, at least, she could be Golda, not Miriam, and her pain might then be singable, made beautiful by the songs, songs she couldn't sing without becoming even more determined that her daughter never forget her mother, her family, her past. She would always be there for her; even now the door was open. It would never not be open, through thick and thin, in good times and bad. Every birthday, every holiday, any time she had a little extra, she sent a greeting card with "I love you" written on the bottom, and a check inside, a check Julie never cashed, and Miriam never stopped sending. That's what a mother does. That's what a mother is. Tradition. Tradition. Just like in the song.

Scene XVI

In the middle of the night, her mother was shuffling to the bathroom when she slipped and fell, breaking her hip. Even Miriam now realized her mother needed more care and supervision than they could give her.

A few weeks later, after Tula had entered rehab, Miriam decided to break the news to her that she would not be coming home, that they had found her a nice place in a nearby nursing home.

When Miriam arrived at the rehabilitation center, her mother's door was closed with a DO NOT DISTURB sign on it. Miriam opened the door a crack, and her mother yelled go away—she was sitting half-naked in her wheelchair while a nurse standing behind her held up one of Tula's arms and sponged it down. With every stroke, loose swags of flesh swayed back and forth, like sheets on a clothesline, and Miriam shuddered. The nurse said it was bathtime and she'd bring her mother out in a jiffy when they were through.

Miriam took a seat in the waiting area beside the nurse's station. The only magazines strewn on the table were on car racing, gardens, or cosmology. She picked up the one with a picture of outer space on the cover, its subject as far away as possible from a human body, and thumbed through it, trying to shake the image of her mother's naked arm, its sagging drapery of flesh. She read about something called dark matter which, "though unseen, makes up more than 90 percent of the mass of the universe." Outside the waiting area, she could hear one of the nurses on the phone, not wanting to be noticed, her voice soft but tense with what it was trying not to sound like, saying, "Honey, listen to me, honey. Honey. Honey. I am not your mother. I Am Not Your Mother." Starlight, Miriam was reading, has to bend around that invisible dark matter, warping itself in order to be seen. "So even after we factor in the distorting effect of time and distance, the light-years of light-years that light has to cross to reach us, the visible shapes we see inside our giant telescopes look nothing like the shapes they are."

On the wall facing Miriam, there was a picture of a white shark hanging next to a muted television on which Miriam saw an aerial view of a funeral procession or a rally—fists were shaking in unison, and if the sound hadn't been muted she would have heard voices chanting, but all Miriam could hear around her was a gauze of medical talk and the occasional soft laugh or cry, and the nurse saying over and over, honey, honey, listen, honey, no you listen, while on the screen she continued looking up at the mass of people who were seething down below the camera like a cell seen under a microscope or, Miriam couldn't help but think, like a dense coating of flies on something dead.

Then suddenly a red car, a convertible, was on the TV screen; it was driving itself down a city street and a black man was running after it and, all at once, he leapt into the air and floated feet first down into the driver's seat and drove away, right to left, as if into the open mouth of the bright white shark.

The writer of the magazine article described dark matter as a black canvas on which the visible universe is painted. That metaphor, the writer said, captures best what he called the paradoxical relationship of gloom to glitter. Miriam wondered if the canvas couldn't also be the painter, the unseen the conjuror of the seen, as if the 10 percent that didn't hide were being imagined by the 90 percent that did.

Dark matter. She was not his mother. She refused to be his mother.

"Here she is," the nurse said cheerily, wheeling her mother, "fresh as a daisy. Time for exercise."

Miriam followed them down to physical therapy where, as usual, her mother refused to participate. They were surrounded by the old, the damaged, the infirm, all working with therapists at different stations in the room. One old woman was looking quizzically at her hand as if it wasn't hers, as it tried to squeeze a yellow ball over and over, only the tips of her fingers twitching while the young black therapist encouraged her the way a mother would, *though she was not her mother,* almost singing, "That's it, Lois, come on now, girl, you can do it, like you did yesterday."

And nearby a man wizened to his very bones held fiercely to the rails of a small track down which he took unsteady small step after small step, like a toddler crossing wet stones—he was followed by another woman who held her hands out ready to catch him if he fell. Everywhere inside the room, the young, the healthy, the fortunate, were helping the old, the sick, the hobbled—everywhere the old, eyes burning, were pushing back with all their might inside their bodies against the dark matter their bodies had become.

Miriam found it beautiful to watch, and strangely hopeful: the room was like a vision of a world, a real world where terrible things did happen, yes, but where the sick desired only to be well, and where everyone who wasn't sick was caring tenderly for everyone who was. But her mother refused all help or comfort, her silence the darkest matter, an impossible density nothing could get around without distortion, broken only by her saying—when Miriam told her about the nursing home and how beautiful it was and how often she would visit—"You are not my daughter, I don't have a daughter, " saying it over and over, as if she knew that Miriam would carry those words and that voice, inside her ever after, beyond rehab and nursing home and funeral, no matter whom she spoke to or where she went, that voice reverberating in her voice, reverberating in the ones she loved, the ones who loved her.

The distorting effects of time and distance. Nothing the shape it was.

Scene XVII

Sam was sixteen when he came home from school one day wearing a cap, a tweed cap, the kind Irish cabdrivers wear. It was three sizes too big.

"Where'd you get that?" Miriam asked.

In a stage Irish brogue, he said, "An old weasel and a young weasel are sitting in a bar; the old weasel says to the young weasel, 'I slept with your mother.' And the young weasel says, 'Dad, you're drunk. Let's go home.' "

"The hat," she repeated. "Where'd you get it?"

"I bought it," he said.

"Bought it? With what? And why? It doesn't fit you."

"With money I saved from running Grandma's errands. And I'm not gonna wear it, Ma, I got it 'cause I like the look of it."

"It's your money," she said. "You want to waste it, waste it. But why?"

He answered with a stupid jingle: "As with my hat upon my

head / I walkd along the Strand. / I there did meet another man / With his hat in his hand."

When Curly saw the hat, he shook his head. "My son, the chemist," he said. "The only person I know who can turn money into shit."

Every day after that it seemed Sam came home with another hat—he had a special fondness for those Irish touring caps, but he also brought home berets, fedoras, an occasional porkpie hat, a Stetson, a bowler—it didn't matter what style, or even what size, whether they were too big or too small, since he never wore them; he only nailed them to the walls in his room. Why? He couldn't say; he just liked the look of them. By the middle of his junior year his room looked like a haberdashery or like a bat cave with hats hanging on the walls instead of bats.

Finally, Curly had had enough of the hats. He didn't care if Sam bought them with his own money; he said the hat buying had to stop. He couldn't stand to see his son waste hard-earned cash. Sam had just learned to drive, and Curly said, you buy one more hat—you hear me—one more, and you'll never use the car again. Never.

It was ten o'clock on a Saturday night in early summer. Sam had taken a girl out on a date. Curly had given him the car. Miriam was in bed reading when the phone rang; she could hear Curly yelling from the den: "You're where? You what? Didn't you lock it? You didn't what? Are you kidding? What are you laughing for, you, you, for Christ's sake!" He threw down the phone and called her to come talk to her idiot son.

"What happened, Sam? Why's your father so upset?"

"Ma," he said, "we went to Harvard Square, see, and well I parked the car and Martha and I, you know, we walked around for a while and then we came back and the car was gone."

"Gone," she asked, "as in stolen?"

"I think so."

"Well, didn't you lock it?"

"I did," he said, "I mean, I think I did."

"You think you did?"

"No," he said, "I mean I know I did. I just . . ."

"Just what?"

"I just think I might not have rolled up the window."

"Oh, for God's sake," she said. "Where are you now?

"We're at the police station. But Ma," and now he's giggling.

"What are you giggling for?"

"Well, you see, there's something else."

"What? What's so funny?"

"Well," he said, "if you think Dad's angry about the car, wait'll he sees the hat I bought."

AT THE END of Sam's junior year, on the Friday night of the big school dance, Miriam opened the door and screamed: "Oh my God, what happened?" Sam was leaning against the doorjamb, eyes swollen and his nose plastered to the side of his face. "Your eyes, your beautiful nose, who did this?"

"Don't get hysterical," Curly said behind her. "It's just a kid fight, right, Sam? No big deal. I hope you gave as good as you got."

"No big deal?" she said. "Look at him, will you? He could have been killed."

"I was dancing," Sam said groggily.

"Dancing? This happened dancing?" Miriam asked, stroking his cheek, leading him inside to the bathroom to clean him up.

"I was dancing with someone's date, might have even been his girlfriend and . . ."

"Did you know she was with someone else?" Curly asked.

"What difference does that make?" Miriam said.

"I did, yeah," Sam said, "when the guy pushed me."

"Serves you right, Sam, when you go after another guy's girl."

"Curly!" Miriam yelled. "You can't be serious."

"Did you push him back?"

"Curly!" Miriam yelled again.

"He's got to stand up for himself, for Christ's sake, even if he is in the wrong. Otherwise he'll become a punching bag for every thug and bully in the school."

"I did try out a little Jewdo on him, Dad."

"Since when do you know judo?" Curly asked.

"Not the J.U.D.O. kind, but the J.E.W.D.O. kind," Sam said with a pained smile. "The ancient art of Jewish self-defense."

"And what is that, exactly?" Curly asked.

"I tried to talk my way out of it."

"Jeez," Curly said, shaking his head. "It's a wonder you're still alive."

"I did get in a few good jabs," Sam added, "but they went over his head."

BY HIS SENIOR year in high school, Sam, too, was hardly ever at home, and when he was, he hardly ventured from his room. He spent hours with the door closed, listening to "music," to Bob Dylan, in particular, to one song, which he played over and over until Miriam couldn't get the screwball lyrics out of her head, something about a kid named Johnny in a basement mixing up medicine, while someone else was on the pavement thinking about the government. Lyrics were Noël Coward, Stephen Sondheim, Gershwin, Lerner and Loewe, but this, what in the world was this? And you call this singing—singing? This was the sound of cats fighting in a Dumpster. And anyway, what did it mean? She would ask him, and he would shrug and say whatever you want it to and close his door.

He was taking creative writing at school, he was studying poetry, of all things. Poetry! Mrs. Pinkerton's revenge! Mrs. Pinkerton, the widow, the walking calendar. Miriam could practically hear her old teacher saying, "Enunciate, girls, enunciate! Expectorate the spuds!" Why did this not surprise her? To make matters worse, he called his teacher, Dallas Alderman, by his first name, Dallas. Since when did that happen? The teacher was barely older than Sam, and with his long hair, work shirt, and bell-bottoms, he was easily mistaken for another student. Sam used to play basketball, but now when Curly asked him why he had stopped, Sam said that organized sports, like organized anything, was too repressive: "Dallas says it's just a dress rehearsal for the military." Curly exploded, "I don't give a shit what Dallas says. Just don't you go and get involved in any politics—you do and I'll disown you like I did your sister. You hear me?" Sam never answered. Closing his door, he'd mumble, "Get dressed, get blessed, try and be a suck-cess . . ."

One day she found a scrap of paper in a pocket of his jeans, which she was taking from the dryer. There was writing on it, but the ink had mostly faded in the wash. Someone whose name began with "M" (the other letters were illegible) was "floating face down in the ego swamp . . ." She found another scrap in the pocket of a shirt. On that, all she could make out was the word "marriage," and, under that, one fragmentary line: "cold shoulder, cold shower, cold storage." On the other side of the paper, something or other, she couldn't make out what, was "like a foreign movie without subtitles." She didn't know what any of it meant (a foreign movie without subtitles indeed!), but she didn't like it, not one bit.

RABBI ALTER CALLED. Did they realize that their son Sam was applying for conscientious objector status and that he'd asked the rabbi for a letter in support of his application? Had they read the application? No, they hadn't. Well, they should.

Sam had made an appointment with the rabbi for early next week. The rabbi suggested that Miriam and Curly come to the synagogue before Sam, so they could sit in the library off the rabbi's study and listen in on the interview.

Rabbi Alter was not your stereotypical rabbi. He wasn't ancient, bearded, and otherworldly. He wasn't stooped with sorrow. He looked like Paul Newman. A dapper dresser with a vaguely patrician affect to his speech (vaguely goyishe, Miriam thought)—everything about him projected worldly success and secular enjoyment. His office, too, was bright, modern, and neat, more like the office of a divorce attorney than a holy man. He ushered them into the library and left the door ajar. While they waited for Sam, they read his CO statement.

They couldn't believe their eyes. Sam presented himself as a pacifist, a pacifism derived from his Jewish heritage, which was laughable given how "religiously" he had avoided stepping foot inside a temple since the day of his bar mitzvah. He refused to go even on the High Holidays. They knew he hated organized religion; organized anything was, in his book, "fascistic." He hated absolutes of any kind (except his own). When they would argue about religion, he would tell them that he regarded God the way Bob Dylan did, as a hypocritical sanction for the basest human impulses, for nationalism, greed, and hatred. Yet here he was fabricating a bullshit religious justification for refusing to fight based on the biblical injunction to treat others as you would have them treat you. What shocked them most of all were the two "conversion" experiences he described, what he called the "turning points" of his spiritual development: when his father decked the drunk before Julie's graduation and when his classmate decked him at the high school dance. But in his version of the events, both Sam and the drunk were portrayed as victims of unprovoked attacks. Not only that, he actually compared his father to "warmongering" America and the stranger to the innocent and noble North Vietnamese. Bad enough that he would lie about what happened, but to malign his father's character like this, to describe him to the rabbi, of all people (and to the government!), as a "short-tempered man who lived by a dangerous code of preemptive justice, a man who swung first and asked questions later, a man whose eye-for-an-eye ethic could only foster conflict, not resolve it," and to do all this in the name of saving his own skin—well, they were speechless with rage and embarrassment.

When Sam entered and sat down before the rabbi's massive desk, it was all Miriam could do to keep Curly from running out and spanking his "spiritual" ass right there.

"So, Mr. Gold," the rabbi said, holding up a copy of Sam's statement, "you're a pacifist, is that right?"

"Yes, I am," Sam answered confidently.

"And you say here," he said, flipping through the pages, "let me see if I can find the sentence, yes, here it is, that your pacifism 'comes from my religious training and my study of the bible . . .' "

"Right," Sam said, not quite so confidently.

"Mr. Gold," he asked, "how many years were you in Hebrew school here at Kehilleth Israel?"

"I don't know," Sam answered, "maybe six years?"

"It's seven," he said. "The exact number is seven. And when you got your bar mitzvah, you were in what grade?"

"Of Hebrew school?"

"Yes."

"I was in third grade."

"So," the rabbi continued, "that means, does it not—correct me if I'm wrong—that you were kept back four years in a row?"

"Um, well, I was never very good at math, but I guess that's right."

"And why," he asked, twirling his glasses, "do you suppose you were kept back four years in a row?"

"Incompetent teachers?" Sam offered with a nervous laugh.

"You know, Mr. Gold, we've never had another student stay back four years in a row, did you know that?"

"No, sir," Sam said. "I didn't."

"Yes," the rabbi went on, "you're something of a legend in these venerable halls. Your accomplishments have not been forgotten." He got up from his desk and took a Hebrew Bible down from the bookshelf. He laid it open in front of the boy.

"Read," he said.

"Excuse me?" Sam asked.

"Read," he repeated. "Read. I want you to read to me, if you'd be so kind."

"But it's in Hebrew," Sam said. "I can't read Hebrew."

"Remind me, then," the rabbi said, "how you managed to read the haftorah during your bar mitzvah service."

"Well," he said, "I listened to a recording of the part I had to read. I memorized it."

"So," the rabbi said, "you went through seven years of school here, stayed back four years in a row, never opened a book in all that time, so that you couldn't read a single word of Hebrew at your own bar mitzvah service, and since that day you haven't stepped foot in temple, have you?"

"No, sir, I haven't."

"And yet," the rabbi continued, "in this document you claim to be a student of the Bible. You quote one line that actually isn't in the Hebrew Bible at all—it's in the Christian Bible—and then you expect me to believe that this so-called pacifism of yours derives from your religious training. Isn't that the phrase you use, 'religious training'?"

Sam scratched his head. "I guess it is."

"Would it be unfair of me to say you have about as much training in the tenets of Judaism as Adolf Hitler? Would it, Mr. Gold?"

"But I consider myself Jewish."

"You're Jewish," the rabbi said, "the way my tie is reddish."

"My sense of humor, Rabbi," the boy pleaded, "my sense

of right and wrong, my connection to family, doesn't all that come from my Jewishness?"

"Dear boy," the Rabbi answered, "it isn't enough just to feel good about being Jewish."

"Who said anything about feeling good?"

"Speaking of Hitler, Mr. Gold, what would you have done if the Nazis had rounded up your family like they did mine and shipped them off to Auschwitz? Would you have fought against the Nazis to protect your family?"

"Yes," he said, "I would, but Vietnam isn't Germany, and Ho Chi Minh isn't Hitler."

"Oh," the rabbi said. "I'm sorry. I misunderstood. I thought you objected to all wars, not just this one."

"Well, sir, I do but . . ."

"Mr. Gold," he interrupted, "there are no buts. You either are or are not a pacifist. You can't be a pacifist only when it's convenient, or when it's safe. Pacifism requires discipline and courage and I would even venture to say a certain recklessness. But you, Mr. Gold, let's be honest now, you—you aren't a pacifist; being afraid to fight doesn't make you a pacifist."

"But Rabbi," Sam said, voice trembling, "can't I object to fighting in a war if I don't think it's just?"

"If you don't think it's just," the rabbi sneered. "You, in all your infinite wisdom, with all your 'religious training.' " He laughed but with no amusement.

"Let me ask you one more thing," the rabbi said. "Has your father read this statement of yours?"

"No," Sam said, "not yet."

"Were you planning to share it with him?"

"At some point."

"What do you think he'll say about how you've portrayed him."

"I don't know," the boy said. "I don't think he'd want me to die in Vietnam."

"Mr. Gold, do you remember the fifth commandment?"

"Not offhand."

"Why does this not surprise me." He sighed. "It's 'Honor thy father and mother.' Do you know what that means?"

Miriam held Curly's arm to keep him from bursting in on them. But when Sam had no answer to the rabbi's question, Curly had had enough and pulled free. Holding a copy of the statement, he walked out into the office.

Sam turned white when he saw him.

"Is this how you see me? Is this what you think of me?"

"Dad, no, I can explain . . ."

"What?" Curly interrupted. "That you see me as a bully? A hothead?"

"No," Sam mumbled, head down, "that's not what I mean."

"Is that how you remember what happened?"

"No, not exactly."

"Not exactly? What does that mean?"

"I mean I do, sort of," Sam said. "I mean, in some ways."

Curly held the essay in one hand, while he slapped it with the other. "You say I charged that guy. You say I hit him for no reason. You don't say that he ran us off the road, that he was drunk, that he was twice my size. You don't say anything except that I swung first."

"But you did swing first."

" 'Cause he was running at me, for God's sake!"

"I'm sorry, Dad, I just . . ."

"Bad enough you write this crap about me," he said, leaning over the boy, who seemed to shrink into himself. "But then to show it to the rabbi, of all people, and who knows who else."

Sam couldn't look up at his father. He was trembling. Miriam believed he'd learned his lesson and wanted the argument to end. But Curly wasn't finished.

"These are lies, Sam. Dirty lies. Do you understand that? Do you have any idea how this hurts me? How embarrassed I am? What did you think you were doing?"

"I don't want to be drafted," he whimpered. "I don't want to go to Vietnam."

"You'll go if you're called," he said. "Like I did. You'll be a man and go."

"That's not my idea of being a man."

"And what do you think a man is, huh?" he asked. "Someone who tells lies about his father? Who humiliates his father publicly to save his own skin? Is that what you're learning in your creative writing classes?"

Curly stood there looking down at Sam. Miriam could see Curly's outrage giving way to sorrow. "I just can't tell you what this does to me, the pain I feel. How could you do such a thing?" He let go of the pages of the essay and they fluttered down around the boy.

Curly walked out. Without turning her head as she followed close behind him, Miriam said, "Be home by dinner."

Sam landed a high number in the lottery; he didn't have to worry about the draft. Like a violent weather front, the sorry business came and went. And none of them ever mentioned it again.

Scene XVIII

Ethan had no business getting married. He was too young, he had to get himself established, make a name for himself, get a few credits under his belt—why tie himself down like that? And to Esther, of all people; Esther, a nice girl, and Jewish, too, but no one cut out for the hustle and bustle of New York, much less for the stage. Esther was all suburbs and bake sales, mah-jongg and bridge clubs, and once she got her claws into that boy he could kiss show business good-bye, Miriam just knew. He'd end up an accountant like Esther's brother, who Sam referred to as "an accountant, yes, but without the personality!" Imagine Joel Grey an accountant, Sammy Davis Jr. an accountant. Fred Astaire, Gene Kelly. What kind of life would that be for Ethan? Was that why she dragged him to Stuart's studio twice a week, year after year, so he could do somebody's taxes? "Let the boy settle down," Curly said. "New York's a tough place; besides, that show business world is full of faygelas, and a wife would keep him out of trouble." Trouble, she thought, Ethan didn't know from trouble. Let him get married, and he'd have all the trouble he could handle.

She said, "This won't end well."

And Curly asked, "Does anything?"

SHE DIDN'T UNDERSTAND Ethan's bitterness and anger. He was struggling, yes, but someday when he was famous he'd look back fondly on these years—he'd laugh about how poor he had been, and about the bit roles and walk-ons he had endured; all of the heartache and disappointment would seem like necessary and invaluable steps on the path leading to his great success. Maybe he was, for now, what he called a "Well-a" actor—the kind of actor who, when he comes onstage, a guy runs up to him and yells, "Hey, where did the cops go?" and he says, "Well, a . . ." and the guy says, "Never mind." End of scene. So what? His time would come.

So what if he made a living off-Broadway, way off-Broadway? Most summers, he did summer stock all over the East Coast, and now and then he landed a commercial. And now he'd just gotten the lead in a new industrial for the jet company Cessna. Miriam needed to remind him that the more he worked, the more people would see him, and the likelier it was that he'd be discovered. She had to take on the task of bucking him up, since Esther wouldn't do it (you didn't need to be a swami to see that coming); Esther was already on his case to grow up and get a real job.

And that was why, even though he begged her not to come, it wasn't worth it, it's grunt work, Ma, believe me, she showed up in Albany, New York, on "opening night" of the industrial, with celebratory roses. Surrounded by an audience of Cessna salesmen, many of whom were drunk and rowdy, whooping and hollering all through the show, she, too, applauded as Ethan came onstage covered in rags. The MC said to the audience of Cessna dealers, "Is this what the market's gonna look like in '73?" And the dealers roared, "No!!!" And the MC roared back, "You're damn right!" He stripped the rags off Ethan, revealing a dapper white tuxedo. Someone threw him a top hat and cane. In the middle of the stage was a trampoline, onto which Ethan leaped and sang, "The market will be jumpin' in '73."

Miriam handed him the roses after the show, in the dressing room, in front of the entire cast.

"Ma, what are you doing here?" he said. "I told you not to come."

"I wouldn't have missed this for the world," she said. "You were wonderful, Ethan. Your voice has never sounded better."

"Good-bye, Cessna," someone in the cast said. "Hello, Ed Sullivan!"

The actors all around them laughed. Ethan laughed, too, but not so heartily.

"Ma," he said, "I got to get changed. Okay?"

"Okay, darling. But you mark my words. Someone's going to hear about this performance. Your break will come. You wait."

As the door closed behind her, she heard the sound of flowers being stuffed into the trash, and someone (was it Ethan?) saying, "I'm ready for my close-up, Mr. DeMille."

Scene XIX

Sam "explained" it to her like this: his poetry professor said his writing had not improved much over his freshman year and what he wanted was for Sam to take a break from writing and just read and not bring him any new poems for at least six months. The professor said for someone wanting to be a poet, Sam was woefully ignorant about the art he wanted to practice. How did he expect to become a poet if he didn't know the history of poetry? So what did Sam propose to do, the schmo, but drop out of school to read! Like they had no books in college! Like college was the last place you'd go to get an education!

So, like a bum, a hobo, he planned to hitchhike to Ohio where he'd move in with his sister and read. What was it Bubbie used to say? "When they're little, they don't let you sleep; when they're big, they don't let you live."

Julie was in graduate school at Ohio State, on a full scholarship, and had a good job in the library. She was still single, as far as Miriam knew, though she could imagine who she might be dating. Now that Sam was living with his sister, it was like they'd formed a separate family. So she had two children she never heard from, though Sam did cash the checks she sent him.

Then a few months later, in the dead of winter, he showed up at the house—hair down to his shoulders, in a long coat that looked at least a hundred years out of fashion. He said he'd moved in with some college friends. He'd be returning to college in the fall. In the meantime, he'd work.

He got a job driving a cab (Miriam thought it must have been the caps still nailed to his bedroom wall that gave him that idea). Then he became a night watchman. He became so enamored of the uniform that he wore it all the time; even after he returned to school, he never took it off. His friends nicknamed him the Watchman. When he'd enter a room, they'd say, "the Watchman cometh." When he'd call, he'd say, "the Watchman speaketh." Was he taking LSD? Miriam wanted to know. He said, "Allen Ginsberg says you should drop acid only if you are at peace in your soul. Clearly acid's not the drug for me."

Scene XX

Her mother died in her sleep in the nursing home on the eve of Sam's graduation from college. Although Tula had once been a very well-off woman, it took every last penny in her estate to cover the funeral expenses.

The last time Sam had visited her, she had said, "So, you want to be a writer? You should hang around here; I'm tellin' you, this is a regular Peyton Place." After graduation Sam moved to Ireland, spending the whole year writing about the family he couldn't wait to get away from.

AT THE END of that year, Miriam and Curly received a telegram from Sam: "Will be home by September; with Irish bride."

Irish bride?

Miriam called him, transatlantic. Sam wasn't really married. He was just helping the friend of a friend who had no other way of getting to America. She'd already been issued one fiancée visa and couldn't get another; so, it was either marriage or no luck. "Once I get her into the States, I'll probably never see her again, so it's no big deal."

"No big deal?" Miriam said. "What happens if she changes her mind and wants you to support her? What happens when you want to get married?"

"Ah, Jaisus, Mum," he said with an Irish brogue that just infuriated her, "she's a good egg, she wouldn't do a thing like that. And as far as me getting married, you know, you and Da"—Da?—"you two blazed a trail too hot for me to follow."

"And what do you plan to do when you return?"

"Oh, didn't I tell you?"

"No, you didn't."

"I got into a writing program out west."

"A PhD program?"

"Not exactly."

"Then what is it? Do you get any degree?"

"No. It's not what they call 'degree conferring.' I just live there and write. It's a writing fellowship."

"I should have figured. How long does it last?"

"The whole time."

"Then what, smart aleck? What'll you have to fall back on?"

"My charm, my good looks, my self-esteem. I'll figure something out. Anyway, you guys don't need to worry about it. After all, I'm a married man."

"Wise guy."

"From your lips to God's ear."

Scene XXI

Miriam thought it was a great idea for Ethan and Esther to move to Los Angeles so Ethan could maybe break into television or film. But as the years passed, LA turned out to be more of the same—auditions, callbacks, double callbacks, promises, bit parts, near misses, the odd commercial, but not much else. Esther was seriously on him now to get out of the business and find what she called a real job. Just as Miriam predicted, she'd been after him for years to grow up and become "a responsible member of society." He had two young girls to feed. He had their future to think of. Lately, when Miriam had called, he'd been depressed and hot-tempered. She couldn't so much as ask about show business without him blowing up at her. Miriam kept repeating, be patient, you'll get yours. I know it.

Then a break came. He landed a big part in the LA production of the musical *Merrily We Roll Along.* He got written up in the *LA Times* as one of LA's up-and-coming stars. He was invited onto the TV show *Fantasy.*

Fantasy wasn't Miriam's cup of tea. She didn't like the "Queen for a Day" segment of it, in which some hard-luck case—some man or woman who'd lost a job, or become disabled, or experienced a death in the family—told their story and then, to great applause, entered the "fantasy booth," a Plexiglas booth full of fake dollar bills into which air was blown. Each guest got one minute to stuff as much phony money as possible into a small plastic bag; whoever stuffed the most money into the bag was that week's winner. Miriam didn't like the way the audience roared while the guest lurched and grabbed at the whirling money. The whole exercise—from the poor me, sad-sack tale to the unseemly money grab—struck her as undignified. Besides, the gifts each winner won (a cruise, a set of golf clubs, a trip to Vegas) weren't going to change anyone's life or bring a loved one back. Unlike her favorite show—*Lifestyles of the Rich and Famous,* where you were guided through a world superior to the world you knew (yes, you envied them, but how else except through envy did you better yourself?)—the point of *Fantasy* was to humiliate the contestants by parading their sorrows on the screen so that the audience could feel luckier than them, more deserving.

But the other segment of the show, the *This Is Your Life* throwback, she adored. An emerging star would be invited on to sing a song or tell a joke, and after the performance he or she would be surprised by the appearance of someone from their past. To Miriam, this was TV at its best—new talent, out of nowhere, got discovered, and family or friends got reconnected.

These were wholesome fantasies, fantasies that made everybody happy. And best of all, her son would be able to showcase his talent to a national audience.

SAM NOW LIVED in Chicago teaching creative writing at a small college. He was beginning to publish widely in reputable magazines; he had a chapbook due out next year.

One day his phone rang.

"Is this Sam Gold, the poet?"

"Umm, yes, I believe it is."

"Brother of Ethan Gold?"

"Yes, that's me."

"Hi, Mr. Gold, this is Shirley Horowitz, producer of the television show *Fantasy.* Maybe you've heard of it?"

"No," he lied.

"Well," she said, "anyway, I'm the producer, and your brother Ethan is going to be our guest."

"That's great," he said.

"Yes, he's going to sing a number from the musical he's in right now."

"Wonderful," he said.

"Yes, it should be. But after he sings, we want to surprise him by fulfilling a fantasy of his."

"Oh, he'll love that."

"We think so. Your brother says he hasn't seen you in a while. Is that right, Mr. Gold?"

"Yeah, it's been a good couple of years."

"Well, how would you like to come on the show and surprise him? You know, be his fantasy?"

"Excuse me?" he said. "What did you say?"

"I said, Mr. Gold, that we want you to be your brother's fantasy. We want you to come on the show and surprise him."

Sam loved his brother and would do almost anything for him. But this, this was too much. He pictured a studio audience, his mother and her entire family in the front row, beaming, as the host intones, "And now Ethan, here's your fantasy, here he is, fresh from Chicago, your baby brother, Sam, the poet!" The audience goes wild, they whoop and clap as the host continues, "And maybe, just maybe, folks, if we really let him know how we feel, he'll share a poem with us, what do you say?"

"Sorry," Sam said, "but no can do."

"Come again," Shirley Horowitz said.

"I can't do it," he said.

"What do you mean you can't do it?" she asked.

"I mean I don't want to do it."

"But you're his brother," she said. "He'll be so disappointed!"

"Did it ever occur to you," he said, "that maybe there's a reason we haven't seen each other in a couple of years?"

"Mr. Gold," she said, patiently, as if to a child, a slow child with a severe learning disability, "your brother's on the edge of stardom here. This could be his big break. Don't you want to be part of it?"

"What about me?"

"What about you?"

"My big break, my shot at stardom, my fantasy."

"I don't know what you mean," she said.

"I always wanted to do stand-up," he said. "You know, like Shecky Greene."

"Shecky who?"

"Or Totie Fields. She lost a leg recently, though, didn't she? So the stand-up part won't work for her."

"What are you talking about?"

"You can't do stand-up if you haven't got a leg to stand on."

"Mr. Gold," she said, "please."

"Okay, how's this? I was so fat I crushed my inner child."

"Mr. Gold," she repeated.

"My wife asked, can I help you off with that? And I was naked."

"Ha, ha," she said. "Very funny."

"I told her I need something looser to wear. She said, 'How about Montana?' "

"Mr. Gold," she said, "I don't have time for this."

"Oh, I've got a million of them."

"Listen," she said, "You're Jewish. I'm Jewish. Let's talk Jew to Jew. Let's have a little J talk."

"A little what?" he asked.

"J talk, Jew talk: J to J," she said. "You mean to tell me that you won't let us fly you out here, all expenses paid, put you up in a five-star hotel, wine you and dine you, and all you have to do is come on stage and hug your brother in front of millions of people?"

"What I mean to tell you is I'd rather have my face epoxied to a urinal."

"Come on, Mr. Gold, get real."

"Real? You want real? I'll give you real, since we're talking 'J to J.' Surely, Shirley (ha ha), you must realize that this is a *real* chintzy fantasy you're giving my brother. If I didn't know you better, I'd say you were J-ing him a little bit. I should be offended. My people should be offended. Moshe Dayan should be offended. I mean, 'J to J,' why not send him to the Bahamas or buy him a yacht, if we're talking fantasy? Me, he can see anytime."

"Okay, Mr. Gold," she said. "Okay, but he'll be disappointed."

"He'll survive. That's what we do, we Jews, we survive. We're good at that."

HE CALLED HIS mother with the news that he had declined the invitation to appear on *Fantasy.* She was frustrated, disappointed, but not surprised. Her son, the foreign movie without subtitles.

Scene XXII

The sirens woke her early one Sunday morning. She could see from her bedroom window the police cars and paramedics in front of Sigrid Rosenberg's house. She hadn't seen Sigrid for a while, but that wasn't unusual. Sigrid would often disappear for weeks or months and then surface again when someone in the neighborhood had died or gotten ill. Sigrid was always there at anyone's side in time of sorrow. She was like the cul-de-sac's official mourner. But for the past several months, since no one had died or fallen ill, there had been no reason for Sigrid to come calling.

By the time Miriam had gotten dressed and gone outside, the paramedics were removing the body in a black body bag strapped to a stretcher. A police officer asked her if she had known the deceased.

"Yes," she said, "I've lived here over twenty years; Sigrid was my neighbor. She used to tie my son's shoelaces."

"She what?" the officer asked.

"Oh, nothing, never mind. I'm sorry, I just . . . can I ask what happened?"

"Suicide, we think," he said.

"Oh Jesus," Miriam said. "The poor thing."

"Does she have any family, any relatives living nearby?"

"None that I know of. She lost her family in the war."

"Thank you, ma'am. If you can think of anyone else who might know something more about the deceased, please let us know."

There was no obituary for Sigrid and, for all Miriam knew, no funeral. When she called Sam with the news, he said he would honor Sigrid by leaving his laces untied for an entire day. He wasn't joking.

Now and then, Miriam had seen Sigrid on the street, and they'd sometimes make small talk, but once Sam had no longer needed Sigrid to tie his laces, Miriam had done all she could to stay out of the woman's way. Sigrid was a carrier of sadness; all Holocaust survivors were. Miriam pitied them, of course, but also felt as if they somehow might infect her with their gloom, as if they judged her for wanting to be happy. Sigrid made her feel as if she had no right to want the things she wanted, as if her dreams were nothing but delusions.

But now that Sigrid was gone, Miriam wondered what she might have done to help her, what signs she might have missed, what cries for help. She tried to recall the last time she had seen her. Was it last month? Two months ago? Did she stop and chat, or just drive by, as she often did, pretending she hadn't seen her calling and waving from her porch? One thing is certain, she didn't know that last time would be, in fact, the last time. Maybe somewhere in her mind she thought, as she drove by, that there was still time, some other time, to give the woman the friendship that she needed. Now it was too late. Sigrid was gone, and now that she was, Miriam couldn't stop thinking about the neighbor she had never liked to see.

Scene XXIII

Miriam decided she wanted to move west, too, to be near Ethan. Curly didn't want to move. He loved Allston. He loved the house. They'd lived there twenty-five years. They'd raised their kids there. All their friends were there. How could she just turn her back on all that history? What about her family? His?

She wanted a fresh start. After Sigrid's suicide, the whole street seemed to be tainted, though what she said was that she couldn't stand the winters. And she wouldn't move to Florida, where so many of her cousins lived—sooner or later, she'd end up taking care of them, too, as they grew old. She'd had enough of caretaking, enough for a lifetime. Everybody's nurse, everybody's doormat; that was her, that was their Miriam. Well, not anymore.

She wanted to be near Ethan, especially now that he was soon to hit it big. And it appeared that Ethan's were the only grandkids they were going to have. She wanted to watch the girls grow up. She wouldn't relent. She threatened to go without Curly. She'd had it with Boston. Against his better judgment, Curly gave in. They sold the house. He got transferred from the Boston Lord & Taylor to the one in Beverly Hills. They moved to Hollywood.

THEY MOVED INTO an apartment complex constructed initially for retirees from the entertainment industry, but now open to the general public. The complex was built around a miniature nine-hole golf course. The units, all done up in a Hawaiian motif, looked out on courtyards, each with a small kidney-shaped pool, artificial grass, stunted palm trees, bronze egrets, and fake aviaries holding exotic wooden birds. Their neighbors were character actors, bit players in old TV shows, the doctor from *Little House on the Prairie,* a cop from *The Honeymooners,* lounge singers, musicians, even a retired Rockette. They lived among the once-almost famous. Their next-door neighbor was an old ventriloquist, who had once appeared on *The Ed Sullivan Show.* He would show up every Sunday morning at their door with a sack of bagels in one hand, and a parrot on his shoulder. "Zei Gezunt," the parrot would say. "How's by you?" On holidays, they held parties and sometimes put on shows in the Aloha Room. Miriam got to sing again, as she had years ago when she had worked for Stuart. Gus Bivona, who had once played tenor sax in the Tommy Dorsey Band, told her she had star quality!

Here, she belonged—right here, where she could live among

the people of her dreams, and where things were really happening for Ethan since the *Fantasy* exposure—he was auditioning for TV shows and movies and commercials.

Not long after they got settled, a film crew shot a scene at their pool right outside their window. It was a Saturday morning. Miriam heard the technicians setting up the shot when she awoke, and she and Curly went out to watch. There must have been ten or fifteen cameramen, not to mention workers building lighting scaffolds around the pool, and the director and his assistants, all with clipboards. Then the two actors arrived with their makeup artists and hairdressers. Other residents had come outside to watch as well. By noon, there must have been fifty or sixty people standing around, waiting for the shooting to begin. Then a young woman with a clipboard approached the crowd. "People," she said, "we need seven or eight of you for extras in this scene; we need some sunbathers in the background—any of you interested?" Everyone, of course, raised their hands. "Okay," she said, laughing. "Okay. Not a shy bunch, are you?"

She picked Miriam and Curly first. Miriam was stunned. Could this be really happening?

Curly said, "I don't know, honey."

"What don't you know?" she said. "What's to know? We're doing this."

And she took his hand and tugged him out to the pool's edge, where the woman had the extras gather.

"All of you get in the lounge chairs and look as natural as

you can, okay? And talk to one another, make small talk, you know, as you would on any ordinary day by the pool."

"But ordinarily we don't talk a lot," Curly said. "We've been married forty years."

"Well, pretend it's only been twenty," the assistant said, smiling. A few of the extras chuckled. Miriam was too excited to notice. "And if you can't think of anything to say, just say 'peas and carrots' or 'rutabagas rutabagas rutabagas' over and over. Start talking when the director signals."

Curly raised his hand, like a grade-schooler.

"Yes, sir," the assistant said.

"Can I keep my visor on?" Curly asked. "My eyes lately can't take the sun. I don't know what the hell is wrong with them, but between the eyes and the leaky bladder, let me tell you getting old's no picnic."

"I'm sure it isn't," the assistant said. "Yes, of course, wear the visor. We wouldn't want to hurt your eyes. Just remember to start talking when you get the signal."

Curly raised his hand again.

"Yes," the assistant said with a sigh. Miriam was mortified.

"Can we move around while we're sitting here?"

"Move around?" the assistant asked. "Like musical chairs? No."

"But do we got to stay in the same position? See, I got a restless leg, drives Miriam crazy. Moves around so much at night sometimes I don't know whether to shit or go blind."

"Sure, mister," the assistant said. "Cross your legs, uncross your legs. Do whatever you like, just stay in the lounge chair, okay?"

So, there they were, seated side by side. Miriam put on her sunglasses. Curly crossed one leg over the other, then uncrossed them, then bent one knee, then straightened it, then bent and straightened the other. When the director signaled, Curly looked over at Miriam and shouted, "Peas and carrots, peas and carrots!"

The director yelled, "Cut! Cut! Hey, you in the visor, not so loud, okay?—you're not hawking vegetables on Hester Street; you're making small talk, background noise. Patter."

"Patter, right," Curly said. "Got a little carried away. First-time jitters."

When the cameras rolled again, Curly said as normally as he could, "Peas and carrots, peas and carrots," and Miriam, staring straight ahead, repeated, "Rutabagas, rutabagas, rutabagas." Meanwhile, at the far end of the pool, the main character, a private eye, approached his ex-wife, a blonde bombshell in a string bikini. He was saying something like, "We'll always have El Paso," when suddenly, to Miriam's horror, Curly stood.

"I gotta go," he said.

The director shouted "Cut! Cut! Now what?"

"Sorry, boss," Curly said. "Gotta go, weak bladder. I'll be right back." As he passed the actors, he raised the tip of his visor to the blonde and winked.

It took three more takes to satisfy the director. When it was over, he congratulated all the extras individually. When he came to Curly, he said, "You're a real character, you know that?"

"Well, I'm always available," Curly said. "You know where to find me."

"I'll keep that in mind," the director said.

Miriam was on cloud nine. That's how she put it in her first letter to Julie from their new address, and in all the notes and cards she sent back east to friends and family. Yes, she missed every one, but LA was truly where she belonged.

The scene itself never made it into the movie, but it thrilled Miriam to think of the two of them being watched by some big-shot producer in a studio at Universal Pictures, to have been captured, immortalized even, in a few frames of a reel in the studio archive.

Scene XXIV

Sam hadn't said anything about a chapbook; it just showed up one day in the mail—thin as a pamphlet. *Family Matters* by Sam Gold. He inscribed it, "To Ma and Dad, love, Sam." On the cover was a picture of a gouged-out block of cream cheese beside a plate of lox. The blade of a knife hovered over the lox. You couldn't see the hand that held it, but something in the tilt of the blade and the splotch of garish light reflected off it told you the person holding the knife was hungry or angry or both.

Miriam had no idea what the cover meant, and the poems, well, the poems were difficult and strange. These were a far cry from the flowery verse that Mrs. Pinkerton had made her recite so many years ago. Though all the subjects had to do with family, she couldn't recognize herself or anyone else in what Sam wrote. The tone was either mocking or sorrowful, and sometimes a harsh mixture of both, but Miriam, for the life of her, could not say why. Where was the uplift? Where was the beauty, the rhyme? Why all the ugliness? People wanted to lose themselves in a book, they wanted to be transported, sung to, just as in the theater. They wanted to be carried away into a better world, into that better somewhere that Maria sings of while holding the murdered Tony in her arms in *West Side Story*. But there was nothing better about the world Sam wrote about. In the poems of his that she understood, the world was messy in familiar ways, in ways all too depressing. She could stub her toe any day of the week. She didn't need to open a book to feel the pain of it.

Curly was having trouble reading lately, so she tried to read a few poems out loud to him, but they never got past the first one because he fell asleep halfway through.

"Too deep for me," he said, opening his eyes and yawning.

"From the sound of it," Miriam replied, leafing through the book, "you'd think he was raised by Nazis in a concentration camp. You'd think we beat him. You'd think . . ."

"Don't worry, Miriam" he said. "It's poetry. No one's gonna read it, and those that do won't get it."

"*Family Matters*," she said, closing the book. "If family matters so much, you'd think he'd call from time to time."

Scene XXV

At last, a letter arrived from Julie, announcing both a marriage and the birth of a little girl. Inside the letter was a snapshot of Julie holding a coffee-colored baby, with Julie's husband looking out over her shoulder, his black face beaming at the camera. In the letter, Julie wrote that she and Sean were happy, and that Danielle, the baby, was the center of their life. She would like her daughter to know her grandparents, but if Miriam and Curly could not accept the three of them with open hearts she never wanted to hear from them again.

Curly threw the letter down in disgust. "The tramp," he said, "the trollop, flaunting it in our faces. Who does she think she is?"

Miriam didn't know what to think or how to feel. She wanted to see Julie and her baby, but she couldn't picture it. What would she say to them? What would they say to her? Sean, whoever he was, whatever he was like, where did he come from? What did he do? What did his parents do? Did he have parents? Was his mother a maid? Had her daughter married Melba's son? How could he not resent her, not hate her? She wanted to show him she was not the monster Julie had probably made her out to be. But she wasn't going to apologize for how she was raised. Julie and all her radical ideals—she thought she could live in a perfect world where everything was the way she thought it should be, and if the world wasn't perfect, she would make it so. Well, Miriam lived in the real world, with real friends, all of whom were raised to think the way she thought. Maybe it wasn't right, but it was too late to change it now.

And yet how could she not respond, not want to see her grandchild? She missed her daughter, she loved her daughter. But the idea of all of them together, one big happy melting pot of a family, that seemed beyond imagining.

That night after Curly fell asleep, she opened an old photo album, on the first page of which was a picture of her and Julie. In the picture Miriam is thin and beautiful. She holds Julie, her newborn daughter on her lap. The baby's fingers are wrapped around her finger; she waves the tiny hand at the camera. Curly sits beside her on the bed. One arm around his lovely wife, he's looking down at his daughter, fussing with her blanket. He seems too shy to look up at the camera. The shyness makes him even more attractive.

She held the other picture up to this one—there was Julie as an infant waving her hand forty years away at her own infant daughter, and there was Julie smiling back across forty years at Miriam who could be her younger sister who's smiling back at her. The fifty-nine-year-old overweight Miriam, her hair dyed blond, looked at the twenty-two-year-old new mother she had been—even in the black-and-white Polaroid she could see how bright her curls were, how smooth her skin. Oh, what a handsome couple she and Curly had made, and how hopefully she had looked out into the future. What would that girl think if she could have seen the future? She would have been appalled to see herself so overweight—she, who'd always been such a beauty, so meticulous about her looks. How had it happened? How had she gotten from there to here? How had that Miriam turned into this one? Sunrise, sunset.

She got out one of the many Hallmark greeting cards she kept, a nonspecific congratulatory card, in which she wrote: "I love you very much." She put a check inside it. Julie never wrote back and, as always, never cashed the check.

Scene XXVI

Ethan quit the business, got his real-estate license, and got a "normal" job, selling office space. Miriam thought that maybe if she reminded him of the world he'd left behind, if she talked show business to him so he wouldn't forget, so it would always be before him, she could save him from making such a terrible mistake, a mistake that someday would destroy the very family he was so anxious to provide for. He'd come to hate his children and his wife if he gave up performing once and for all, couldn't he see this? Couldn't Esther? He would say, "Get off my back, Ma. Leave it alone." But when she wouldn't leave it alone. When she raised the subject every time he called or visited, when she cut out the latest reviews of shows in which this or that old friend was starring, when she showed him the reviews, when she said, "See? See? They struggled, too, and now look at them," he would just explode. He would scream, "It's not about you, understand? It's not your life, it's mine!"

Curly would tell her to back off, stop nagging him, she was driving the kid away. But she couldn't do it. She wouldn't do it. She couldn't bear to see him ruin his life by throwing away something he loved so much.

Nagging? He was standing in the middle of the freeway and a truck was hurtling down upon him. She wasn't nagging. She was pulling her child out of harm's way just in the nick of time.

THEN, A FEW years later, it happened just as Miriam had predicted: after almost twenty years of marriage, Ethan, the happy family man, walked out on his wife. He had come to resent Esther for pressuring him to give up show business, and when she finally couldn't take any more of his tantrums and sulking and told him to go back to the stage if that would make him happy, never mind about her and the kids, he tore up his real-estate license and began auditioning again. And when he landed a role in the Broadway-bound musical *Sunset Boulevard,* he decided that he was done with Esther, with Hollywood (his girls, after all, were nearly grown), and that he would move to New York for good. He told his mother he'd made all the sacrifices he could make. Life is short. You've got to seize whatever opportunities come your way. One of the opportunities that had come his way happened to be a young woman in the cast of *Sunset Boulevard,* with whom Ethan had fallen in love, but this part of the story he kept to himself, for now. Miriam felt terrible for Esther and the two girls, but she was thrilled for Ethan. Esther had never truly supported Ethan's love of show business. She had badgered Ethan into real estate, and in doing that she drove him out. It was her fault for not appreciating him. Terrible and painful as it was to see the marriage fail, Miriam nonetheless believed that this was for the best, not just for Ethan, but for all of them. In the long run they would all be happier. In the short run, no one was happier than Miriam. She would be there on opening night to celebrate with Ethan. She couldn't wait.

CURLY WAS CERTAIN Ethan must be gay, to walk away from a wife and two children after so many years. He blamed it all on Miriam and that faygela Stuart Foster. When Sam would remind him that Ethan and Esther had fought constantly and had never seemed especially happy, Curly would say, "Happiness and marriage, that's like comparing apples and, and, and—horseshit."

JUST BEFORE HE moved to New York City, Ethan introduced them to Alice, his fiancée. Curly was relieved that Ethan was a man's man, even if an irresponsible one. Miriam was thrilled. Alice was tall and willowy and had a strong, high voice. They looked so good together. And boy, with those long legs could she dance. They might become a famous duo—like Steve and Eydie, or Fred and Ginger. Alice could give him the encouragement he had never gotten from Esther. Now maybe he'll have a fair shot at stardom. For once in his life, maybe he'd catch a break. God knows, the boy deserved it.

ACT
III

Scene I

He couldn't remember the lyrics. He'd get into an audition and start to sing "I've Grown Accustomed to Her Face," or "On the Street Where You Live," or "Maria," songs he'd been auditioning with forever, and suddenly he'd draw a blank. No words would come. He thought it must be stress. He'd been through a lot the last few years—the divorce; Alice; Esther's unrelenting fury and incomprehension; the constant traveling between New York and LA to see his children. The divorce had been hard on them. But they'd get over it; they'd see eventually how happy he was now, how good this would end up being for all of them. Besides, he'd been getting work, bigger and better roles; things were turning his way, at last.

But then he couldn't remember where he lived. He couldn't recognize his own address when he saw it on an envelope. Words longer than two syllables he couldn't pronounce. He couldn't even remember the words to "Happy Birthday."

They operated on the tumor the very day it was diagnosed. Glioblastoma multiforme. Prognosis: maybe a year.

Miriam thought, Why me? When she spoke to Ethan, though, she said, "Think positive." She said, "You can beat this." She said, "The glass is half-full," and "What doesn't kill you makes you stronger." It infuriated him how she refused to accept his situation. She argued with his terror. She tried beating it to nothing with clichés, bromides, platitudes. Her belligerent optimism, her desperate good cheer—she set his teeth on edge. Whenever she called, Alice would answer. She would say that Ethan was sleeping. Miriam was no dope. She noticed that Ethan was always sleeping when she called.

A FEW MONTHS later, in July, he came down with meningitis. The tumor hemorrhaged. His left side was paralyzed. A nurse was helping him from the bed to the commode when she lost her grip and dropped him. He was wearing his *Sunset Boulevard* T-shirt—the T-shirt he got the cast to sign for him when he left the show a year before the cancer. As he fell, the nurse grabbed for the T-shirt and it ripped off. He was apoplectic. The phone rang. It was his mother. The nurse handed Ethan the phone, not knowing what else to do. He tried to tell his mother what had just happened, but all that came out was, "Fucking bitch . . . Fucking bitch."

Miriam thought he was yelling at her. She yelled back, "You can't talk to your mother like that. Who do you think you are?"

He stammered, "No. No. You . . ."

"No, you," she said. "You listen to me. I'm your mother and you'll treat me with . . ."

"Shit," he said. "You don't . . ."

"No," she interrupted. "You don't, you don't talk to me like that, I don't care how sick you are."

He slammed the phone down. Miriam was beside herself. She was in a rage. When Sam called, she started right in, no hello, how are you—just "He can't talk to me that way. I'm his mother, and he's got to learn to treat his mother with respect."

Sam said, "Ma, he doesn't have to learn anything anymore. He's done with learning."

And she said, "Not if I have anything to say about it."

IT TOOK A month of physical therapy before he regained all his motor skills. Toward the end of this period, he became oddly cheerful. Maybe it was the crisis atmosphere, the show of love from all his friends, all the attention he was getting, but when Miriam and Curly flew in to see him there was a weird party atmosphere in the apartment; he was like a different person, happy, calm, attentive to others, like he didn't have a care in the world. Miriam thought it must be the chemo he was undergoing. Well, whatever it was, they should all be thankful. Happiness was happiness, let her son just be happy, please God, even if under such terrible circumstances, even if only for a little while.

On that first night, Alice's dog, Daisy, bit Miriam on the

hand. Miriam had been cooking dinner for everyone. Daisy, a high-strung border collie, was following her from stove to counter, from counter back to stove, in the hope of something falling from a plate or dish. Miriam pulled the brisket from the oven and stepped on Daisy's paw. The dog yelped, Miriam nearly dropped the brisket. A little gravy spilled on the floor. Daisy scrambled back over the tiles to the gravy. Miriam yelled, "Get away you—get get get!" But Daisy didn't get, and when she tried to push her away, Daisy bit her right through the oven mitt. She didn't break Miriam's skin, but the bite was hard enough to bruise her. Miriam came running out of the kitchen, holding her hand, screaming, "What kind of meshuggene dog is this!"

"Miriam," Alice said, gently, trying not to laugh, and tending to the already swelling hand, "you make her crazy when you yell like that. Just speak to her in a normal voice."

Curly said under his breath so everyone could hear, "That was her normal voice."

"Just keep her away from me, okay?" Miriam said.

Ethan laughed, "Leave it to you to bring out the attack dog in Daisy."

Curly patted Daisy on the head. "Good girl," he said. "Good girl. Welcome to the family."

YES, HAPPINESS WAS happiness, but Alice was worried that Ethan wasn't facing up to the gravity of his situation. She didn't like it that he didn't complain, now that he could walk and talk again and wasn't in any kind of pain; besides the occasional nausea, he wasn't breaking down or blowing up. Alice was afraid that when the symptoms returned, as they surely would, and everyone was gone, it would be so much worse for him if he didn't prepare himself for it now while the family was here. "To hell with reality," Miriam told her, "he should just be happy while he can." But Alice wouldn't let it go. She said that the family still had a lot of unresolved "issues"—since when was family an issue, like crime or welfare? Yet Alice went ahead and arranged for a therapist friend of hers to facilitate, for Ethan's sake, what she called a family session.

So HERE THEY were, facing each other in Ethan's small apartment; even Sam had flown in for the session with Belinda, their therapist for the night, an attractive woman in her early forties. She had bright blond hair teased up into a breathy supernova. Curly took one look at her and muttered, more loudly than he meant, "Sweet Magnolia, how high is your hair!"

Miriam had never met anyone so professionally earnest—like an actor acting the part of a therapist. She spoke in short clauses and so slowly it was as if she thought that English was their second language.

"Okay," she said, "let's begin. I so admire you all. Let me say that first. I admire you for agreeing to share your feelings. This is a very difficult time. A painful time. It's hard for even the closest of kin to talk openly about the death of a loved one. It's so much harder to do so in front of a stranger. A crisis like this brings up a lot of ancient history, buried emotions, forgotten wounds. Honesty is risky. Things get said. Things get said and people get hurt. When people get hurt, they shut down. When people shut down, the hurt festers. When the hurt festers . . ."

"What the hell is she talking about?" Curly blurted out.

Belinda seemed not to notice. "See," she continued, "anger is a secondary emotion. There's always pain behind it. So my job as facilitator is to help you all get past the anger to the pain, so you can hear the pain. So you can listen to it with an open mind. And speak with an open heart. Okay? Okay. So, what I'd like to do first is to go around the room and have each of you say what you hope to get out of the session."

She turned first to Curly sitting to her left. He was still staring, dumbfounded, at her hair. He looked like he wanted to reach up and touch it.

"Mr. Gold?" she said.

"Yes," he answered.

"Would you like to go?"

"No thanks," he said. "I went a little while ago before we all sat down. I'm fine for now. But I appreciate you asking."

"No," she said, "I mean, would you like to say anything to us, to Ethan."

Curly just stared back at her.

"About tonight," she continued. "You know, what you hope to accomplish here tonight."

"Accomplish?" he asked.

"Dad," Sam said, "is there anything you want to say to Ethan?"

"I did already," he said.

"When? How?" Belinda said. "You haven't said anything yet."

"Earlier," he said. "Before you got here. In private."

"Would you like to share with us what you said to Ethan?"

"What, are you kidding?" he said. "That's family business."

"But this is family therapy," she said.

"Yeah, sure, but I mean family as in, you know, father and son. As in personal."

"But that's what therapy does, Mr. Gold. It delves into intimate things like that, the more personal the better."

He said, "But there's personal, and then there's personal. This is the latter, if you know what I mean, not the former."

Belinda scanned the room for help. "Would anyone else like to start?"

"I guess I will," Ethan said. "I hope after tonight we can feel a little closer to each other."

"Since when aren't we close?" Miriam asked.

"I'm not saying we're not," Ethan said.

"What are you saying then?"

"That there's room for improvement."

"We're a family, not a house," she said. "You need us, we come. You're sick, we take care of you. What's to improve?"

"Ma," Ethan said, sighing. "You don't have to get defensive; no one's attacking you."

"I'm not defensive!" she said. "Why do you say I'm defensive? And how is it not attacking me to call me defensive?"

"I'm just saying . . ."

"I'm making a point," she interrupted. "Can't I make a point?"

Belinda jumped in, asking if any of them could change one thing about themselves, what would it be?

Curly, staring at Miriam, said, "No comment." Sam joked that there was a particular hat, a boater, he wished he'd bought back in the day, but when no one laughed, he said he could do a better job staying in touch and maybe be less driven by his work. Ethan said how much he's come to value truth and honesty and that he wished it hadn't taken cancer to make him see the light.

When it was Miriam's turn, she stared out at the room, saying nothing, her jaw clenched.

"Mrs. Gold," Belinda prodded, "is there anything you'd change about yourself, your life? Anything you wish were different?"

"You mean aside from having a son I can't keep from dying and a daughter I never see?"

Nobody said anything. Nobody, especially Belinda, knew what to say. Then Ethan, tears running down his face, dropped to his knees, and on his knees walked over to Miriam. Like Al Jolson, she thought, he looked like Al Jolson singing "Swanee how I love ya' how I love ya.'" She almost laughed, but then he reached up for her hands, and he said, "Ma, I'm begging you, open up a little, for once in your life. If my illness is telling us anything, it's that we don't have time for bullshit."

"You think what I did for you, the sacrifices I made, were bullshit?"

"No, Ma," he said. "Just that you never really . . ."

"Don't you lecture me," she said. "Don't any of you dare lecture me. I never did anything but what I thought was best for you, for every one of you, and I never asked for anything in return except respect. I wasn't perfect? Sue me. I did the best I could. And now I have to watch my son die. So nobody gets to tell me how I'm supposed to feel."

The very force of her outburst seemed to lift Ethan to his feet and push him back across the room into his chair.

"Well," Belinda said, smiling, looking around the room, "does anybody have anything else to add?"

No one had anything else to add. She thanked them, she said she hoped the evening was "cathartic." She commended their courage and honesty and she wished them all the best in the days ahead.

Miriam was furious. Miriam had never been so furious. She was seventy-five years old. She had done the best she could, and what good would it do now anyway, to think she could have done more of this or less of that? Why rake through the past for this or that shortcoming or failure, since the past was what it was, and nothing could change it? She had plenty to complain about, too, but did she complain? No, and why? Because she knew what happened when you vented your feelings—you just had more feelings to vent.

EVERYONE (BUT JULIE, of course) was at the hospice: Ethan's fiancée, his daughters, his brother, Curly and Miriam. Alice was reading a profile of Ethan by the Broadway star Gwen Salsby in the latest Actors' Equity Newsletter. Her letter was a warm and detailed tribute to Ethan. Ethan, she said, was not only a fabulous performer, but also a tireless fighter for actor's rights, serving many years on the union board. He had helped to establish and publicize the Actors Fund, which was designed to help defray the medical costs of unemployed actors. He was diligent, hardworking, a joy to be around, a model of professionalism and dedication, somebody everybody in the business knew and admired. She invited the union, all fifty thousand members, to join with her in thanking Ethan for his service to the art, and in Ethan's name to donate something to the Actors Fund.

By the end of the letter, his daughters were crying; his father sobbed.

Miriam said, "It's a shame, Ethan, you were never famous."

What was wrong with everyone? Sam and Curly were shaking their heads, the way they did on the opening night of *Sunset Boulevard* when she had shown how disappointed she was that Ethan hadn't landed a bigger role in the show. And Ethan, Ethan was looking up at her the way he had so many years ago, whenever she'd forced him to go to Stuart's, or when they'd visited her father and she had asked him to perform, to sing a song for his grandpa—he was looking at her with such hatred you'd have thought she'd given him the cancer. What had she said? He had so much talent, more talent than almost anyone, and if life were fair, he'd have gotten what he had worked so hard for, what he deserved. Was that such a terrible thing to say? Why wouldn't anyone look at her? Only Ethan looked at her and his look said, what kind of monster are you? It must be the tumor, she decided, those drugs he's taking. Her poor boy.

She said, "Honey, can I get you something? Are you thirsty?"

He just rolled over and said nothing.

From then on, he was always sleeping when she was there.

SAM HAD TAKEN Curly back to the hotel, but Miriam hadn't been ready to leave yet. She had been at Ethan's bedside all day, every day, for the past three weeks, even though everybody had begged her, Alice especially, to take a break. Three days ago, the nurse had said Ethan could go at any moment. So at the end of each of the past three days, Miriam had said good-bye to Ethan, as if for the last time. Something in Ethan's uneven breathing and the way the tip of his tongue peaked from the corner of his mouth told her tonight would be the last night. On the windowsill, there was a vase holding a single iris, at the top of which a bud was on the verge of opening into a purple blossom. Outside the window, under an enormous elm tree, a nurse on break was smoking a cigarette, pacing back and forth outside the front door of the hospice. Beyond her and the circular driveway, cars were passing by in both directions, red lights running into white lights, white lights into red. What day of the week was it, a Friday? If so, many of the people in those cars were no doubt heading out for the evening, to dinner maybe or to a movie. How many children would be conceived tonight? How many would be born? Sunrise, sunset. Swiftly flow the years. As the nurse paced, the tip of the cigarette burned like a wayward star. Her uniform was incandescent under the dark leaves. Behind her, Miriam could hear Ethan's ragged breathing. She could sense the flower's machinery pumping water up through the stem into the bud, the water changing invisibly, moment by moment, into petals, into fragrance, the fragrance wafting out into the night where somebody, maybe the nurse down there, still pacing, would breathe it in with the raveled threads of smoke. It was obscene how beautiful that budding flower was; how sweet it soon would smell, how bright the nurse's bright white uniform was against the darkness. It was outrageous that there were people anywhere not mourning. It was absurd and stupid that her son would be dead by the time the flower broke into bloom. Miriam grabbed the arrogant little stalk of it and threw it in the trash. She called Sam to tell him she was ready to go; he should come right away to pick her up.

It was one a.m. when Sam returned from the hospice with the news that Ethan had died. The vigil was over. Curly broke into sobs. Miriam said nothing. She pulled a chair to the hotel window. She sat, staring out at the black night. Sam threw some blankets on the floor. Curly got into bed. Wouldn't it be funny, Sam thought, if tonight of all nights he wet the floor and had to get in bed with his parents? But it was a king mattress, not twin beds. There'd be no crack. No place for him to sleep.

When he woke, he found Curly still asleep in bed, and Miriam still sitting in the chair, staring out the hotel window. "Ma," he said, "do you want some breakfast? Can I get you anything?" She didn't answer. She didn't move. All day she sat there, staring out the window of the Holiday Inn.

JUST BEFORE THE service was to begin, the funeral director approached the family.

"Before we start," he said, "we have one last piece of business. I'm so sorry. I should have had you do this when you arrived. But before we can close the casket, someone in the family has to identify the body. It's just a formality. It won't take a second."

Miriam said, "Sam, you go do this. I just can't do it, and you know it's too much for your father. Go with the man, please."

Sam came back, ashen. "Are you okay, dear?" Miriam asked, but he just sat there, staring straight ahead, saying nothing.

The service was beautiful. Ethan's daughters both spoke about Ethan as a kind and devoted father, how funny he had been, how much they'd miss him. Several of Ethan's show business friends gave testimonials to Ethan's unforgettable voice and his charismatic stage presence. Miriam wasn't amused by the funny stories they told of his short-tempered personality, but she savored every compliment, every remembered instance of his generous heart, his loyalty, his comedic gifts. Miriam wanted Sam to speak; he was the writer in the family, after all, but Sam refused. He sat beside Miriam without expression, off in his own little world, as always.

As they were filing out of the funeral home, Sam disappeared into a side chapel. The limousine was waiting out front to take them to the cemetery. This was no time for his shenanigans. She told Curly she'd be right out; he should tell the driver she'd be just a minute.

Sam was sitting in the back pew off to the side, slumped over, his face in his hands. His sobs reverberated in the chapel. When was the last time she had seen him cry? She put her arm around him.

"Honey," she said, "come on now, we have to go, the limo's waiting."

"He was waxy, Ma," he said. "He was cold and waxy, like a wax statue, like a mannequin."

Miriam shivered. Suddenly it was sixty-five years ago and she was in the back room of her mother's shop, surrounded by bald-headed plastic bodies.

"And the hair was all wrong, it was combed down over his forehead, like he was hiding a bald spot or something—and the mouth, the lips, they were all wrong, it wasn't him, it just wasn't him. Didn't you give them a picture?" Now he looked at her. There was more rage than sorrow in his face. She couldn't speak.

"Why did I have to do it?" he said. "Why me?"

"Do what?" she asked, not knowing what else to say.

"That should have been your job. Not mine. You don't ask a child to do a thing like that."

"But you're not a child, Sam, you're a man," she said.

"That," he said, pointing back behind him, "that thing in there—how am I going to see anything but that from now on when I think of him? How am I going to get that image of him out of my head?"

"No, darling, no," she said, and he stiffened as she tried to pull him closer. "You'll see him; you'll see Ethan, your brother, as he was, as he really was, on a stage singing and dancing."

"Remains to be seen," he said, and laughed without amusement.

"What?" she asked.

"I'll see a corpse," he said.

When she didn't reply, he added, "You're right, Ma, though, about one thing: I'm a man. I've always been a man; I was never a child."

"No, that's not what I meant," she said, choking back her own sobs now. "You're my youngest, my baby."

"I was never a child," he repeated.

"What do you mean?"

"It doesn't matter," he said. "What can it matter now?"

"Oh, darling," she said. "I'm sorry. I'm so sorry." And now his resistance slackened as she pulled him close. He was like a boy again, a child. When was the last time she had held him like this, her baby? Had she ever done so? Was there ever a time? "Oh, darling," she repeated, her voice now hoarse with sorrow. "I'm sorry; I'm so sorry for everything." And they sat like that together until the funeral director came to tell them that the limos were waiting; it was time to go.

• • • • • • •

Scene II

• • • • • • •

She had one knee replaced. Sam flew out to California to look after Curly while Miriam recuperated. Curly was nearly blind now, incontinent, and the Parkinson's made his hands shake so badly when he ate that most of the food ended up on the floor. Most of what he spooned into his mouth was air.

The night Sam arrived, each separately complained to him about the other. According to Miriam, Curly was and always had been a tightwad, a penny-pincher, a skinflint, who cared more for his meager savings (what he inherited from his perfect father!) than he did for her. He haggled over every expenditure; he made her feel guilty and irresponsible for buying even basic necessities. He hated to travel, hated to go out to dinner. God forbid, she shouldn't have to cook one night! He would never do anything for her. As his eyesight had worsened, she had taken over paying the bills and keeping records, but he nagged her constantly about what they had, how much she was spending. Whenever she talked with anyone long distance, he hovered by the phone, pointing to his watch to remind her how much the call was costing. He refused to believe her when she'd say they had unlimited minutes on the weekend or in the evenings, the only times she ever made long-distance calls. He was self-absorbed and pig-headed and wouldn't put himself out in even the smallest ways to make her life easier. He refused, for instance, to sit down when he peed. Just refused to do it, no explanation or justification offered. He'd stand because that's how he'd always done it, never mind the mess he made or how bad the apartment smelled, or how much trouble it caused her, having to clean up after him, day in, day out. What had he ever done for her?

"You know, your father—he's never loved anybody but himself," she said. "He never wanted to go and do like my girlfriends' husbands. I couldn't complain about it without him saying, 'Go write your Bosnian pen pal,' or 'Thank your lucky stars we're not in Baghdad.' But what does it say about your life if the only way you can feel good about it is to think 'at least I'm not in Baghdad.'"

So what if it's worse for other people somewhere else? She's not other people. Unfortunately, neither is he.

ACCORDING TO CURLY, Miriam took good care of him. Boy, did she ever. She was two-faced, a phony, all "darling this" and "darling that" when others were around, but a regular Bride of Frankenstein when it was just the two of them.

He knew he was a handful, but what could he do? Was it his fault he had gotten old and sick? Besides, she'd been complaining about him for as long as he could remember; what had he ever done for her? what had he ever done for her? What *hadn't* he done, that's what he wanted to know. He had worked like a dog, he had paid the bills, she had made nothing working for that faygela Stuart; he had bought her a good house, a car; he had never cheated on her, had never beaten her. What the hell else did she want?

LATER THAT NIGHT, Sam was helping his mother down the hallway to the bedroom. They passed the guest bathroom. The door was open. There was Curly standing at the toilet. He was looking down, shouting at his penis, "Piss you, goddamn it, piss!"

She called out, "Who are you talking to in there?"

He called back, "No one you would know, sweetheart."

She laughed all the way to bed, where the pain in her knee would keep her up all night.

ON THE FIRST Passover after Ethan's death, Sam visited his parents again. Curly slept most of the time. Miriam was so overweight, she couldn't stand up without panting and sweating. She wouldn't let anyone help her prepare or serve any meal, not even breakfast, though she complained constantly about having to do all the work herself. Afterward, she wouldn't let anyone help clean up. Instead, she panted, she sweated; like her mother, she said, "Oy Gottenyu," as she hobbled around; she said, "I'm tired of taking care of everyone. Your father, he should be in a nursing home already." Curly started to cry. She told him to forget it; he wasn't going anywhere. They couldn't afford it, anyway. Now she was crying, too.

The apartment complex held a luau in the Aloha Room. As Miriam and Curly entered, their neighbor Sabina came up to Curly and put a lei around his neck. She said, "Curly, do you want a lei?" And he said, "Boy, do I want a lay!"

• • • • • • •

Scene III

• • • • • • •

The poetry reading was supposed to start at four thirty. That was the time he had told her. She had written it down. She had gotten directions. She and Emma, Ethan's youngest, had gotten there at four fifteen. Now it was four thirty-five, the room was nearly empty, and Sam himself had only just arrived. She had never been to a poetry reading before, except for the choral recitations back in high school, which she had hated. In fact, she'd never actually read through any of his books. Oh, she was proud of his achievements. She bragged about him to all her friends. She kept his books out on the coffee table for all to see. But the truth of the matter was, his poems befuddled, enraged, or depressed her. She hated the way he wrote about the family, and her, in particular. He would find so much "significance" and "complexity" in moments she remembered (if she remembered them at all) as being meaningless, or happy in a simple, uncomplicated way. Everything he wrote about was tinted with gloom or anger. Nobody, not even Sam himself, came off as especially attractive. People she knew, herself included, were depicted with warts and all, living lives that were a far cry from everything she had once wanted to see on the stage. Nothing he wrote about could she imagine in a musical—how do you sing about bedpans, hospices, the Holocaust?

But never mind what or how he wrote—she couldn't stand the fact that he, and he alone, got to present her to the world; she had a right not to be written about, didn't she? Didn't she at least have the right to control how she'd be described? Yet let her suggest, however gently, that he got this or that detail wrong, and he'd get all Mr. Fancy-Pants Professor on her (as snooty as Mrs. Pinkerton!) and go on about "the truth" and how she wanted to deny it, wanted to live in an "airbrushed" world. Some defender of the truth, he was. What about that CO essay he had written years ago—how much respect for the truth did he show in that? "Facts," he'd say, "I'm not talking about facts when I talk about the truth. I'm talking about my experience of facts." But facts were facts. If he found out that Helen Keller had only been near-sighted and a little hard of hearing, wouldn't he call her book a lie?

And even if some of what he wrote about was true, did it ever occur to him that there might be some truths worth denying? She'd never gone around telling the world he'd been a bed wetter—for all she knew, maybe he still was; maybe that's why he had never married. Mr. Don't-Write-About-Anything-But-The-Truth, why haven't you hung out that piss-stained laundry?

But, God forbid, she should suggest that maybe everything didn't have to end up in a poem, and suddenly she's no better than the Nazis. Still, someone must like his work enough to publish it, to give him a job because of it, and to invite him to a fancy university, all expenses paid, to read it to people probably just as depressing as he was.

She had never seen her son "perform." She had always imagined that a reading would be like an off-Broadway play, only smaller, a little kookier maybe, a dimly lit, smoky room of beatniks snapping fingers while a Maynard G. Krebs look-alike chanted gibberish ("floating face down in the ego swamp").

A few more people wandered in — the seats were filling up. It was four forty-five now. No one seemed in a hurry to get things started. If it didn't start soon, it would take her hours to get home on the 405, it would be stop-and-go the whole way. This would never happen in the theater.

Sam came over. He was wearing a tie and jacket, which was good, and a surprise to Miriam, but the jacket looked like it had been slept in by a wino, and the tie was stained and rumpled. A Beau Brummell he wasn't.

"Ma," he said, "you got here all right."

"When are we gonna get this show on the road? I've been here since four fifteen, and the traffic's gonna be murder by the time we get outta here."

"Ma," he said, "it's not my call."

"I'm just sayin,' a show's supposed to start when a show's supposed to start."

"Well, I have to say hello to a few people. I'll see you afterward."

"Break a leg," she said, smiling. "Or is it break a line?"

It was five o'clock when he began to read. Everything Ethan was as a performer, Sam wasn't. Sam fidgeted, he scratched his head, he adjusted his glasses. He couldn't keep still, like he had ants in his pants. Worst of all, he made no eye contact with the audience; he hadn't memorized his lines—instead, eyes glued to the book, he read. He read too fast. He mumbled ("Expectorate the spuds!"). It was like he couldn't wait to get this over with—which in a way she appreciated, considering the traffic—but, still, he could use a little polish, a little training. He didn't know the first thing about commanding the stage; he didn't know how to work a crowd. When he finished the first poem, he looked up at the clock to check the time. He finished the second poem, and again he looked up at the clock. She couldn't contain herself.

"Stop lookin' at the clock!" she barked.

He looked around, flustered, as if he couldn't believe his ears, as if he must have dreamt what he had just heard. Was that . . . could she have? He read another poem. When he finished, again he glanced at the clock, and again she called out, "Enough with the clock already. Buy a watch!"

He was fifty years old and his mother was telling him how to give a reading. He was being heckled by his mother! He picked up the pace. He finished the reading in record time. It was clear to everyone he couldn't get away fast enough. The mild applause hadn't yet abated when she said, "You're a big boy—why don't you wear a watch?"

He leaned down and hissed, through clenched teeth, "Ma, this is not the time."

"How would you know?" she replied. "You don't wear a watch."

A few hours later, he called to make sure she had gotten home all right. She said, "Sam, let me give you some advice."

"Uh, Ma," he said, "listen. I appreciate it, I really do. But I'm afraid we won't be any closer after you give me the advice than we are right now. So I'll take a pass, okay?"

"Suit yourself," she said, clearly miffed. "It's your show."

Scene IV

Curly was sitting on the end of the bed in his boxers, staring at his feet, waiting for her to help him get his socks on. He hadn't put his teeth in yet, and the sunken lips made him look older and frailer than he was. He looked like an old man, any old man, like Father Time. It made her feel old and frail just to look at him. She was thinking, either I'm dressing him, feeding him, cleaning up after him, or undressing him. No one had told her the golden years would be the color of piss.

"Come on, Curly," she said, "pick your feet up a little so I don't have to bend over so far."

Slowly he looked up at her. He opened his mouth. What came out was, "Ma . . . Ma . . . Ma . . ." He couldn't lift his arms. He couldn't stand. A dumb smile on his face.

At the hospital, he had suffered another stroke. He couldn't speak at all now. He couldn't swallow. Movement had returned to his arms; just like her mother had, so many years ago, he kept trying to pull out the IV, or the catheter, or the feeding tube, so they put the big mitts on his hands. He pawed impotently at the tubes and wires; he thrashed his head from side to side, his eyes wide with pain and confusion, looking at Miriam as if to say, what the hell is happening, why can't you help me? And then, when the distress subsided, he seemed lost in hallucinations. His eyes were following something above him, and now and again he raised his hand as if to point, as if to say, look Miriam, look, can't you see? See what? she wondered. Ethan? Who is it, Curly? Who do you see?

Sam, of course, was the only person in America who refused to buy a cell phone. He said he couldn't stand how everyone walked around talking to people who weren't there, each the Caesar of an invisible empire—declaring through a bluetooth: I text, I fax, I phone. He called them cell-ots.

She had left messages on his home phone, letting him know what had happened, telling him to come as soon as possible. Would it kill him to check his messages once in a while?

THE FOOD THEY were feeding Curly through the feeding tube was giving him terrible diarrhea. And they wouldn't give him anything for the pain, because sedatives and such would alter his brain chemistry and make it difficult for them to measure his "progress."

Progress? He's barely conscious, Miriam thought.

She asked the neurologist what the prognosis was.

"If you mean for a full recovery," he said, "not very good."

"What kind of recovery are we talking about, then?" she asked. "Will he ever get out of bed? Will he talk again?"

"Listen," the doctor said, "he wasn't in great shape to begin with. He was malnourished and frail. And the chances of him regaining what he's lost aren't good. Not impossible, but not good."

"What about coming home?"

"Probably not." He shook his head.

"So what, then, does rehab mean?"

He said he was sorry, but he didn't really have an answer for that one.

"Well, doctor," she said, "what you're telling me is that my husband will spend the rest of his life in bed, a vegetable in a nursing home."

"He'd be alive."

She heard herself saying, "I want you to pull the feeding tube. I want you to give him something for his pain. I want you to . . . he should only just be comfortable. He's eighty-seven years old. He just shouldn't suffer, not if he can't get well."

"Does he have a living will?" he asked.

"Yes," she answered. "It's in his file."

"What you're asking for is that we stop treatment. You understand that, don't you?"

"Yes."

"And that we move your husband to hospice?"

"Yes."

"Okay, then. If that's what you want."

If that's what she wants? The little pisher, what does he know from want? She had been taking care of Curly for seventeen years. For seventeen years, a bowl of cherries it wasn't. She couldn't go anywhere; she couldn't spend any time outside the apartment without disaster striking—he'd knock over something, he'd forget to take his pills, he'd soil himself. Day in, day out, she cleaned up after him; she cooked, she cut his food, she picked his food up off the floor, she dressed him, she changed his diapers, and lately changed the sheets every morning, like she had to do for the boys when they were little. And what did she get in return? Did he care how he put her out? Did he ever so much as thank her? And now what? He goes into a nursing home which they can't afford, and every day, every single day, she's there, visiting, because how could she not? Right there, every day, the devoted wife he couldn't stand and couldn't do without, until either he drops dead or she does. Want? She's eighty-one years old. Sixty-three years they've been married. She's tired. She's buried one of her children and lost another. She has a right to be tired. She doesn't have anything to prove to anyone. The good daughter, the good mother, the good wife, and where did it get her? Want.

When the doctor left, she took Curly's hand and said, "Darling, we're gonna move you to a nicer place where you'll get well. We're gonna make sure you're comfortable." Then she took his dentures from the glass on his bedside table and put them in his mouth. "There, sweetheart," she said, "now you'll look just like yourself when they come to get you."

FINALE

What should she do with Curly's teeth? She can't bring herself to throw them away, but it feels somehow inappropriate, even creepy to keep them. The pink and yellow dentures float in an aqua-colored plastic container the hospice nurse handed her the day after he died—she'd returned to his room for his radio, toiletries, and whatever else of his she'd overlooked in her haste to leave the night before. Taped shut, "Hank Gold" scrawled on top, the container now sits on the end table next to her recliner. She takes the dentures out from time and time, astounded, baffled that such an intimate part of him should now feel cool here in her hand. She can almost see his mouth and lips materializing around the upper and lower incisors, the darker canines and the molars echoing his jaw, the upward sweep of his cheeks. Even the gums, colored a dull brownish pink so like the tones of an old man, her old man, nearly make his wry smile visible, so that the more she stares at them, the more she wants to hear his voice say, "No one you would know, sweetheart."

Funny how if he were alive, she wouldn't notice them at all. They'd only be his teeth. She has distributed her pictures of Curly and his jewelry to the grandchildren. His clothes she sent to the Salvation Army since Sam didn't want them. The radio she's keeping for herself. But his dentures—what should she do with them? Maybe send them to Sam. They're just the sort of thing he'd want.

ONCE THE YOUNGEST of her family, she is now the matriarch. Her cousins have long since died. Her nieces and nephews and their children (and theirs) have scattered across the continent; some of them she hasn't seen in years; most of them she's never met. Like a crumbling empire, the family has broken apart as it's expanded. But she's the matriarch and she alone, it seems, resists as best she can this process of disintegration. Her means of resistance is the greeting card.

At the beginning of each year, she goes to Hallmark to buy cards for everybody in the family, on both sides, from Julie to surviving cousins, nieces, and nephews, down to grand- and great-grandnieces and -nephews, and cousins three or four times removed. She even sends cards to Ethan's ex-fiancée, Alice, and if Sam would just remember to give her his Irish "wife's" address she'd send her one, too. She buys birthday cards, anniversary cards, and holiday cards. Because you never know, she also buys a sizeable number of condolence cards and thank-you cards, and cards for showers, births, and illnesses.

She steers clear of the jokey ones, the ones full of sarcasm and lewdness. She likes the old-fashioned ones, the ones with sprays of flowers on the outside, and gold calligraphic lettering, and on the inside little rhymes that express thoughtful feelings, the general kind, the kind that anyone would or ought to feel on this or that occasion. She likes cards that do her feeling for her, so there's nothing left to write except "Love, Miriam."

When she gets home, she signs the birthday, anniversary, and holiday cards in advance; she seals, stamps, and addresses them, then places them in a file divided into months and weeks. Every Monday, she checks the folder for that week's recipients and mails whatever cards she finds.

Whenever Sam tells her he's going to a particular city, she says your cousin so-and-so is there, you need to look her up. And he says, "Why would I do that?" And she says, "Because she's family, that's why."

Sam once told her, "You know, Ma, what the difference is between us?"

"I can't wait to hear."

"You're a federalist when it comes to family feeling, whereas I'm more of a tribalist."

"I have no idea what you're talking about."

"For you," he says, "family is family, no matter what. For me, some blood is thicker than others. After you, Dad, Julie,

Ethan, and my nieces, there really isn't anyone in the family I care that much about."

"And if you cared so much about me, how come in all these years you never send a card on my birthday?"

SHE'S PACKING UP in preparation for the move back east, to be near Sam. Far back in the hall closet, she finds the mahogany memory box—the mother's day gift she received from all three kids way back in the sixties. Inside the box, she finds the card they gave her: a picture of a nun on the front, with a caption inside that reads, "To a superior mother, if not a mother superior." Under the caption Ethan wrote, "All my love and respect. You are always in my heart. Your middle one, Ethan." Under Ethan's signature, Sam wrote, "No, Ma, Ethan never loved you. I loved you. I was the only one who ever loved you." And under his signature, Julie wrote, "No, Mom—Sam & Ethan are incapable of love. It is only I who love you."

SAM PULLS UP to the front of the retirement home twenty minutes early for their weekly lunch; she's sitting outside on a bench, next to the front door, ready to go. How long has she been sitting there in the cold, he wonders, sighing. She's breathing little angry streaks of steam.

"You're late," she says.

"What do you mean late?" he says. "I said be here at one; it's not even a quarter to."

"It's close enough to one; I've been waiting out here since twelve fifteen."

"Out in the freezing cold? You're gonna kill yourself."

"You should have thought of that before you kept me waiting."

She settles into the car and sighs the sigh that says "some life."

"Have you talked to anyone today?" he asks.

"Who's to talk to?" she says.

"Grandchildren?"

"They'll call later," she says. "Probably sometime tonight."

"No one from Boston?"

"No."

"So what's new?"

"They're raising my rent another eighty dollars. I'm now paying over two grand a month. Can you believe it?"

"How's your money holding out?"

"What can I tell you?" she says, with a shrug. "Even with the Social Security checks and dividends, I'm basically living off my principal. But the way I figure it, I have enough to last me eight more years."

"You'll be ninety," Sam says.

"Ninety," she repeats. "I'm ready to go right now. Either way, I don't want my money to outlast me. I want to outlast my money."

"If Dad weren't dead already," he says with a laugh, "he'd drop dead hearing you say that."

"And look where it got him," she said. "Used to drive me crazy how he worried over every goddamn cent. 'What, are you gonna be buried with your bankbook?' I used to tell him. Like talking to a wall. 'Can't sell my father's stocks,' he'd say. 'My legacy this,' he'd say. 'My legacy that.' And I'd say, 'Is that gonna make you any less of a dead man?'

"Eight years," she repeats, shaking her head. "Eight years. Funny thing, when you look back, eight years is nothing, it's like the bat of an eye, but when you look ahead, it's a pretty long stretch of time."

Sam says, "The years fly by, but the days are long."

"What?" she says.

"Nothing."

"I mean, if the doctors had figured out a way to give Ethan another eight years to live, he'd have felt like he'd won the lottery."

At the restaurant, she says, "Did I tell you I had a bit of a to-do with a lady at lunch the other day?"

"What happened?"

"It was no big deal really. I was sitting with this woman, Margaret Whitfield, a nice lady, you know, pleasant, we were talking about this and that, and I asked what's going on with the search for a new chef, and she pointed at a table near us and said, 'Oh, the Jews over there, they took it over.' I didn't know what to say, I was so flummoxed, but it ate away at me, I had to do something, so at supper that night when Margaret sat down at my table, I said, 'Margaret, you might want to sit with someone else.' And she said, 'Why, Miriam?' and I said, ''Cause I'm a Jew, and you don't seem to like Jews.' 'Why do you say that?' she asked, and I said, 'Because of what you said at lunch today.' She said, 'Oh I didn't mean anything by that, I love Jews,' and then she said, get this, 'Some of my best friends are Jewish.' Can you believe it?"

"What did you say?"

"What did I say? I said some of my best friends are goys. And we laughed. Listen, so we won't be best friends. I can still eat lunch with her."

"Hey, I have some news, too," he says after a moment. "Good news and bad news."

"Give me the good news first."

"I heard from my wife."

"And what did the Mrs. have to say?"

"Well, she's back in Ireland, been there for years now."

"Terrific. Tell me her address. I'll send a birthday card."

"Yeah, not only that, she's married, my wife, and has three kids."

"Is that the bad news?"

"Not exactly."

"You never told me you got divorced."

"We didn't. She got the marriage annulled."

"How long ago?"

"I don't know, maybe ten, eleven years."

"Why didn't you ever mention it?" she asks.

"What, so you can start nagging me to marry. Anyway, that's the good news."

"And the bad news?" she asks.

"The bad news," he says, "is that from now on, I can't say anymore that I've never cheated on a single girlfriend. Not even with my wife."

"So why don't you find a nice girl and settle down already? You're no spring chicken." And now she laughs, "I'm not gonna be around forever."

"Me, neither," he says. "I'm married to my work, Ma. And anyway, I'm more a love 'em and leave 'em type of guy. Sometimes I forget the love 'em part and cut straight to the division of property. As Dad would say, it's a life, even if it ain't much of a livin'."

"Maybe if you settled down, and this time with a Jewish girl for a change, your work wouldn't be so gloomy. You remember, Sam, what your grandmother used to say, 'You wanna be a writer, get married; it's a regular Valley of the Dolls!' "

"Peyton Place," he says.

"What?"

"Peyton Place. Not Valley of the Dolls. And she wasn't talking about marriage but the nursing home. She said the nursing home's a regular Peyton Place and that maybe I'd write a best seller if I hung around her a little more than I did."

"She was right about that," she says. "You could've dropped in to visit her from time to time. That wouldn't have been so terrible.

You were always her favorite. But Peyton Place, Valley of the Dolls, what's the difference? The point is you could have a wonderful life—I mean you got your health, a house, a pension—it wouldn't kill you to get married, and maybe then, who knows, you might write something cheerful. Come to think of it, it wouldn't kill you to write a best seller either."

THE RESIDENTS TAKE a day trip to the area's Museum of Art. Miriam was never much of an art buff or museum-goer. Paintings either bored her with all the Christian nonsense, Christ-this or Mary-that, or they made her squeamish with all the nudity. And then there was the modern abstract stuff she didn't understand or like. Standing in front of triangles or circles, or dull blocks of color, she couldn't shake the feeling of being caught in a joke and laughed at, as on that old TV show *Candid Camera.* She glanced scornfully at every canvas, as if to say to the invisible cameraman that no one was going to make a fool of her, try as they might.

This museum is no different from the others she's visited. But one piece in the contemporary section does capture her attention. It occupies an entire wall, an enormous white canvas almost covered over in black squiggles, and number-like shapes. The painting, if that's what it is, looks like something by that Jewish painter from the fifties, a canvas filled with wriggling lines and curls—like a swimming pool full of worms. When she steps up close, she sees that the lines are names, and the numbers are dates, they're signatures, each bearing its own distinctive loops and flourishes, its own particular day and year—names and dates written beside, beneath, over, and on top of names and dates, each one in another's way, each one obscured by others. Some of the names are smudged beyond recognition, some seem to be disappearing back into the canvas, some seem to push up against the names beneath them in order to be read, and they would have been if not for the names that in turn were pushing against them.

But even the most faded or obscured, when focused on individually, seems certain of attention, hopeful; each curve or line, slanted forward or back or perfectly balanced, each self-important little dot, if taken one by one, seems like a fantasy of worth that all the other fantasies over and around it cancel out. A mysterious sorrow rises within her from she doesn't know where. She could be hurtling through outer space, between stars and beyond stars, out past the farthest galaxy, the whole visible universe behind her shrinking now to nothing but a dim speck in the blackest night.

Tears running down her face, she can't look away until the activity director, touching her arm, says, "Come on, Miriam. It's time to go."

MIRIAM DOESN'T REALIZE that Catherine Olsen, the woman across the hall, is losing her mind till she starts showing up two or three times a day in Miriam's apartment, not knowing why. A retired high school English teacher, genteel, soft-spoken, but always a little flustered, as if startled by everything, Catherine always asks, "Oh my, you didn't call me, did you? You wouldn't know what I'm doing here?"

One morning Miriam is straightening up a little before going down for breakfast when she hears something behind her and turns to find Catherine standing in the doorway of the living room.

She jumps when she sees her. Her surprise surprises Catherine who steps back and says, "Oh my, I'm sorry. I just . . ." She is wearing an old cardigan, her arms folded, her fingers fretfully pulling at the frayed edges of the sleeves.

"Can I help you with something, Catherine?" Miriam asks.

"No, no," she says as always. "I'm not sure. Maybe. I don't know."

"Would you like some tea or coffee?"

"Oh my, no, of course not." Then she chuckles, "My goodness, the thought of you making tea for me. That's rich."

Miriam has no idea why that is rich, but she laughs as if she does. Catherine is looking around the room, at the books in the bookcase, at the desk scattered with bills and coupons.

She inspects the bookcase, running her finger down the spine of book after book. She says, "I started a book club here when I first moved in, but now I can't remember a single book we ever read. I miss it, though, the talk, the socializing. You're a reader, aren't you?"

"Oh well, you know, sometimes."

Then Catherine goes over to the desk and examines the papers strewn across it. She leans up close to the computer screen and squints at the lines. Then she stands there, confused, trying to think of something. She looks around at all the things, the couch, the end table, the coffee table, as if some object might recall what it was she's come here for.

Finally Miriam says, "Um, Catherine, if I can't help you with something, I really would like to get back to work. I have a few things to do before breakfast."

"Oh, of course, dear," she replies, mortified. "I'm so sorry for the bother. I just don't understand what's happening to me."

Every day after this, Catherine appears unannounced in the living room, confused about how she's gotten there, certain she's come on some important errand she cannot recall. Miriam, of course, is annoyed at first but after a while she doesn't mind the intrusions. She even looks forward to them. She likes being needed again. Almost like being a mother.

One day, Catherine notices on the coffee table one of Sam's poetry books. Miriam had told her more than once that her son was a published poet. She had often shown her the very book she's holding now. This time Miriam doesn't say "Only my son's" when Catherine asks, "So, you read poetry, too?"

As Catherine rambles on about her years of teaching high school, Miriam finds herself thinking how terrible it must be to feel your mind disintegrate, to be aware of the disintegration yet unable to do anything to stop it. She pities Catherine, this frail, handsome, helpless woman. And then finds herself recoiling from the pity. After all, she is several years older than Miriam. And from what Miriam has gathered, it seems that Catherine has had a relatively happy life. Her daughter visits her once a week. She often brings the grandchildren with her, though they never stay very long. Once or twice a week, a late-middle-aged woman picks her up and takes her somewhere for the afternoon. Before and after retirement, Miriam imagines that Catherine's life has been a happy one. She has money—she can tell that from the clothes she wears and how she speaks—her husband must have been successful, and like most couples they must have traveled everywhere. They must have done things together. And her daughter, God, her daughter seems so happy to see her every week, her daughter seems to really enjoy her mother's company. Her daughter is part of her life.

She remembers how, when Ethan was dying, she couldn't see a homeless person in the street and not think, "Why the hell do they get to live and my child has to die, someone with so much good to offer to the world?" She never likes the thought, she knows it isn't fair, but still she can't stop thinking it, just as now one moment she finds herself feeling sorry for this distraught, befuddled old woman, anxiously at loose ends, seeing herself die piecemeal, day by day, and the next moment she thinks, wait a minute, the hell with you, what about me?

One day Catherine invites Miriam for tea, though when Miriam arrives, Catherine doesn't remember having invited her. She is wearing nothing but a bathrobe and her hair is unbrushed and wild.

This is the first time Miriam has been inside her apartment.

The living room is small, like Miriam's. Family pictures adorn one wall: in what seems like the oldest of them, Catherine as a young woman stands beside a tall man Miriam assumes is her late husband. He's wearing a white suit and a straw hat—a boater (Sam would have loved that one); he has one foot on the fender of a 1940s Buick that looks spanking new, and one arm around his handsome wife. Through the trees behind them there is lake water, and white sails on the lake. Next to it is a picture of Catherine holding a baby in one arm while her free hand rests lightly on the baby's stomach. She looks contentedly into the baby's face. Her daughter. Her beautiful daughter who visits every week. Miriam studies the infant face as if its sheer contentment, sleeping in her mother's arms, might tell her something about her own child, her daughter, and where she is and why it is she never wants to see her mother. She looks from picture to picture, from birthdays, to anniversaries, from holiday to holiday, vacation to vacation: the girl grows up, marries, has children, and the children grow from babies to toddlers, toddlers to boy and girl, and then her husband ceases to appear in any of the pictures, and in all the ones remaining with her daughter and her daughter's family, Catherine looks out at Miriam, confused, distraught, as if to say what difference does it make what kind of children you have, or who your husband was or where he did or didn't take you, you still end up like this.

Miriam points to the picture of her and her husband posing

nearly sixty years ago, before that brand new Buick. "Is that your husband? Were you two on your honeymoon?"

"My what?" she asks.

"Your husband."

"My husband," she says, mystified. "My husband. I should think I'd know who my own husband is."

Holding her own arms, Catherine begins to pick at the threads of her frayed robe. She looks at Miriam without seeing her, she looks like a panicked child abandoned by her parents, in the middle of a strange city. Miriam shudders.

Not knowing what else to do, she takes Catherine by the arm and leads her to the bedroom and sits her down at the dressing table in front of the mirror. Catherine looks at the frightened and disheveled woman looking back at her. "Let's fix your hair, dear," Miriam says. "Maybe you should do hers first," Catherine points at the mirror. "She needs it more than I do, I should think." The sight of that other woman seems to calm her down. Miriam takes a brush and runs it through the wirey hair. She sees Catherine's face in the mirror and her own hand resting on Catherine's shoulder, while her other hand brings the brush down over and over. She sees Catherine's face tighten in discomfort and then relax as the brush works gently through each kink, snarl, and tangle until after a while there is no resistance. Miriam brushes and keeps on brushing. Catherine closes her eyes and starts humming to herself a melody Miriam knows but can't quite identify.

She doesn't realize she has closed her own eyes, too, until she hears Catherine say, "Thank you, dear, for coming by. We simply don't do this enough."

"Is there anything I can do for you since I'm already here?"

"No, dear, no," she says. "I think I may lie down. I don't know why I'm suddenly so tired."

LATER THAT EVENING, on her way out for supper, she finds Catherine in the hall with her bathrobe open, and only one slipper on her foot, her eyes frantic, her cheeks flushed. She has soiled herself. Her legs are streaked with shit. Miriam's eyes burn with the stench. "Catherine," she says softly, one hand on her elbow, "come inside, darling; someone might see you. You don't want to be seen like this. Come, let's clean you off."

"I can't, it seems, oh dear, you wouldn't know where I am, would you?"

"Sure dear, you're home, at Emerald Shore, you live here, across the hall from me. I'm Miriam, remember?"

"Are you my daughter?"

"No, dear, I'm your friend, I'm Miriam. I'm your neighbor."

"I should think I'd know my own address."

"Come, I'll show you. Here, this is where you live. Here, in this apartment, right across the hall from mine."

Miriam leads her inside into the bathroom where she takes off her soiled robe and nightgown, and gets Catherine in the shower. She slips out of her housedress and underwear and enters the shower, too. There is no other way to get her clean. It can't be helped.

How small Catherine is, not much bigger than a child, an ancient child, with flat dugs, and wrinkled thighs and belly. Gently as she can, she runs the washcloth over Catherine's front and back, and between her legs. Her hands are diffident at first, uncertain, shy, but Catherine oohs and ahhs with pleasure, like a little girl, a child, being bathed by her mother, and then begins to sing in a high fluttery voice: "The water is wide, I can't cross o'er, and neither have I wings to fly, give me a boat that can carry two, and I will row my love and I." Was that the song she was humming earlier? Water runs down both of them now, loose gowns of water flowing over their faces, Miriam can hardly see what she is doing, but she doesn't need to see; it is like the older woman's body leads her hands where they need them to go, where the hands themselves need to go but don't know it till they get there; Miriam doesn't think about her children and the nights now more than half a century away when she would bathe them briskly and efficiently, eager to get them into pajamas and off to bed so she could have a little time alone. She doesn't think of Curly and the chore of washing him those last hard years, the unresponsive body so male, so heavy, so resistant to her will. She doesn't think child or mother, wife or daughter. She doesn't think at all. It is like her name, her history, and everything that makes her who she is has been washed away with the shit and piss. She is just one creature, hobbled and old, washing another creature, even older and more hobbled, and even after there is only a soapy fragrance all around them, she continues to draw the washcloth everywhere over the other body in rhythm to the song the other sings.

A few days later, the manager informs the residents that Catherine has been moved to an acute care facility and will not be returning to the community.

EACH MORNING, NO matter how poorly she has slept, or how tired and achy she is, or how often she's told her son that she wants to die, Miriam makes her bed. She smoothes out the bottom sheet, then spreads the top sheet over it, then spreads a blanket over that and pulls tight, tucking in the corners; then she fluffs up the pillows, and over the pillows and the mattress drapes a comforter, which she pulls, pats, and neatens until the bed, revealing no trace of her tossing and turning, looks brand-new, like a showroom bed in a fancy store. Hungry or not, she eats a little breakfast, unconsciously, insensibly, a cup of coffee and a piece of toast, and then she thumbs through the paper, does the crossword puzzle, and afterward washes the cup and plate and wipes down the counter until it's immaculate.

She makes herself presentable because she always has done so: she puts on makeup, does up her hair, chooses what dress or shirt and slacks to wear, and which accessories. At lunch, she sits with Charlotte Voss, a new resident, who moved into Catherine's apartment, and whose husband, too, has recently passed away, whose daughter had died from cancer many years ago, and whose son is a computer whiz.

Sometimes during lunch, while she and Charlotte trade stories from the past, Miriam feels as if they're characters in a play, performing themselves; it's like she's floated out of her body into a ghostly audience where she watches these two old ladies, these charming and poignant "old potato pickers" (that's what Curly would have called them), each taking turns telling stories, each appearing to listen to the other until it's her turn to tell the story she's calling up inside herself the entire time the other speaks. Miriam tells her about her successful mother and her husband, who had been so good-looking as a younger man; she tells her about Ethan and his theatrical career, his unforgettable voice, and how, if only he'd gotten this or that break, just once, so much of it is luck, how big a star he would have been. She tells Charlotte about Julie and how smart she is, her political passions, her job as director of a major university library, the various degrees she's earned, and about Sam and his childhood quirks and eccentricities, the tucked-in shirts, the shoelaces, the hats, she should have known from day one he'd turn out to be a writer. And what a poet he's become. And such a good boy, a real mensch. He takes good care of her. She even talks for the first time about Stuart and what a way he had with the piano and the shows they put on together and how good he was with Ethan. Telling stories now to Charlotte, she feels as if her past is something that had happened in another world, not just another time, more like a dream than a play she's only now recalling, a dream that hardly had to do with her at all. What a musical it would have made. A hit, for sure.

After lunch, she reads in her recliner or watches her soaps. Sometimes she goes back to the dining hall for supper; sometimes she doesn't bother. She misses Catherine. She misses Catherine terribly, but will not talk about it, not to anyone. What good would it do? Everyone's got trouble enough, she thinks. What was it Bubbie used to say? "Oh my little shayna punim, don't be so sad—someday you'll see if everybody put their troubles down on the sidewalk, so you could see them, you'd pick yours up and run." No, she won't make a fuss. She won't have anyone feeling sorry for her; she'll go as always to the poker game on Tuesday nights and on Wednesday nights to bingo. She'll sit with her friends and kibitz, because that's what she does, that's who she is. Nobody will say "poor Miriam" when her name is mentioned.

AT BEDTIME SHE folds back the comforter, folds back the blanket and top sheet, and gets into bed, the arthritis in her back, her hands, her hips, promising another restless night, resulting in another painful morning, when she'll nonetheless drag herself up and make the bed and eat and make herself presentable and tell her son "How should I be?" when he calls to ask her how she is.

I want to thank several dear friends and family for help with this book over the many years that it evolved: Pam Durban, Daniel Wallace, Tom Sleigh, and my beautiful and brilliant wife, Callie Warner. I need to single out two friends in particular, Jill McCorkle and Allan Gurganus, without whose insight and encouragement this book would never have gotten to where it is. I also want to thank my agent, Janet Silver, for her wise counsel, on and off the page, and my editor at Algonquin, Chuck Adams, for his faith in the book and his indispensable guidance.

BROADWAY BABY

Life vs. Art: A Note from the Author

Questions for Discussion

LIFE VS. ART

A Note from the Author

In both my poetry and my prose, my personal life has been a source of subject matter. But in saying that, I feel it's important to point out that personal experience is not art, and art is not personal experience. For one thing, personal experience does not happen in sentences and paragraphs, or lines and stanzas. For another thing, even in a story that follows closely something that may have happened in life, the writing of that story always requires a selection and arrangement of detail, and thus is always as much invented as recalled. While autobiographical detail often finds its way onto the page, my loyalty in writing poetry and fiction (nonfiction is another matter) is to the story itself as it evolves, and not to the actual events that may stand in back of this or that scene or stanza. In *Broadway Baby,* for instance, I have drawn on certain facts of my personal life. Like Ethan, my brother David was a Broadway actor, a song and dance man, and like Miriam's parents, my mother's parents were divorced in the 1920s. My family lived at the same time and in the same place as the Gold family in the novel. And like Hank Gold, my father spent most of his working life running his father's slaughterhouse. But while some external facts are similar in some ways, the internal lives of the people in this book are completely imagined. What they think and feel and often what they do issue from the dramatic necessities and pressures of the story as it unfolds. The story itself determines how the characters develop. I took my cues from what was happening on the page, not from anything that has happened in the world. And even where there is some correspondence between real and imagined life, that reality is transformed into art, into linguistic forms and patterns that I hope illuminate experiences that otherwise, in the world itself, are muddled and confused.

Why do essentially good though complicated people behave in ways that can have damaging effects on both them and those they love? How do people survive devastating losses? In times of trouble, how do the things we desire become as much a refuge as a passion? In what ways are the dreams we dream as much a burden as a blessing? How do we see past our fantasies about other people to develop a real appreciation of who they are? These are the questions I aim to explore in all my work. My need to ask such questions may derive from the particular circumstances of my life, but the exploration itself is governed by imagination and the necessities of art.

QUESTIONS FOR DISCUSSION

1. In the Broadway show that Miriam sees, *Showboat*, the character Miss Julie is a kind of outcast after she is exposed as being born of mixed blood, an anathema in the period in which the musical play was set, right after the Civil War. Why do you think the ten-year-old Miriam identifies so closely with the character of Miss Julie in particular, and to the lure of the stage in general? What is it about her family life and her parents' divorce that predisposes her to love the theater, to dream about a life on stage?

2. By means of musicals and Miriam's lifelong love of them, what does this novel say or imply about the role not just of entertainment but of art in general, high art as well as popular art, in how we live our lives?

3. How does Miriam's relationship with her mother, Tula, influence the kind of mother she herself becomes?

4. Despite her dreams of stardom, Miriam is in many ways a conventional middle-class Jewish housewife. How do those conventional values shape her relationship to her children, to her daughter Julie's involvement with African Americans, to Sam's eccentricities and his later passion for poetry, and to her friendship with Stuart Foster?

5. While Miriam is anything but a religious Jew, how does her Jewishness inform her understanding of the world? Why do you think she is made so uncomfortable by the presence in her neighborhood of Holocaust survivor Sigrid Rosenberg?

6. Why is intimacy, physical as well as emotional, so difficult for Miriam? What in her makeup or in her cultural and historical background hinders her from connecting with her children and her husband? Does she ever realize what it is about herself that estranges her from others?

7. In their last conversation, Stuart Foster tells Miriam that she's been living in a dream world. In what ways is this statement true? In what ways do Miriam's dreams, hopes, and expectations cut her off from those she loves?

8. Faced with a distressingly dysfunctional home life, Sam retreats into a world of his own creation, using biting humor rather than overt rage as a coping mechanism. Discuss the very narrow lines that separate comedy from tragedy and humor from anger. Given his upbringing, do you envision a happy adult life for Sam? Why or why not?

9. Miriam loses her daughter Julie to the culture wars of the 1960s and her son Ethan to cancer. She cares for her mother, Tula, when she falls ill; she cares for Curly during his long physical and mental decline. In what ways do these catastrophic losses change her? In what way do they humanize her?

10. At the end of the novel, there is a moment of redemption for Miriam, a moment of seeming uncharacteristic humanity and love. The moment involves the character Catherine Olsen—what is it about this woman that draws Miriam to her? How does Catherine help Miriam overcome her inhibitions, her squeamishness about the human body?

11. Do you feel that Miriam was a "good" person? Which of her traits and characteristics do you relate to, and which do you find most unattractive?

12. The lack of emotional interaction between members of Miriam's family is a constant theme in the novel and leads to frequent conflict, yet in the telling, the story is full of humor. Do you find this kind of "black comedy" an effective way to convey the reality of human emotions, or do you think the story would have been more effective if played "straight"?

CALLIE WARNER

Alan Shapiro is the author of ten volumes of poetry and two memoirs, one of which was a finalist for the National Book Critics Circle Award. He has received a *Los Angeles Times* Book Prize, a Lila Wallace–*Reader's Digest* Writer's Award, and the Kingsley Tufts Poetry Award, among other honors.

Other Algonquin Readers Round Table Novels

The Frozen Rabbi, a novel by Steve Stern

Award-winning novelist Steve Stern's exhilarating epic recounts the story of how a nineteenth-century rabbi from a small Polish town ended up in a basement freezer in a suburban Memphis home at the end of the twentieth century. What happens when an impressionable teenage boy inadvertently thaws out the ancient man and brings him back to life is nothing short of miraculous—as is this brilliant novel.

"[A] wonderfully entertaining, inventive new novel that evokes Amy Bloom, Michael Chabon and Isaac Bashevis Singer . . . Laugh-out-loud funny, the sort of humor that takes you by surprise." —NPR.org

AN ALGONQUIN READERS ROUND TABLE EDITION WITH READING GROUP GUIDE AND OTHER SPECIAL FEATURES • FICTION • ISBN 978-1-61620-052-7

A Blessing on the Moon, a novel by Joseph Skibell

Hailed by the *New York Times* as "confirmation that no subject lies beyond the grasp of a gifted, committed imagination," this highly acclaimed novel is a magical tale about the Holocaust—a fable inspired by fact. Not since Art Spiegelman's *Maus* has a work so powerfully evoked one of the darkest moments of the twentieth century with such daring originality.

"As magical as it is macabre." —*The New Yorker*

"Hugely enjoyable . . . A compelling tour de force, a surreal but thoroughly accessible page-turner." —*Houston Chronicle*

AN ALGONQUIN READERS ROUND TABLE EDITION WITH READING GROUP GUIDE AND OTHER SPECIAL FEATURES • FICTION • ISBN 978-1-61620-018-3

A Friend of the Family, a novel by Lauren Grodstein

Pete Dizinoff has a thriving medical practice in suburban New Jersey, a devoted wife, a network of close friends, an impressive house, and a son, Alec, now nineteen, on whom he's pinned all his hopes. But Pete never counted on Laura, his best friend's daughter, setting her sights on his only son. Lauren Grodstein's riveting novel charts a father's fall from grace as he struggles to save his family, his reputation, and himself.

"Suspense worthy of Hitchcock . . . [Grodstein] is a terrific storyteller."
—*The New York Times Book Review*

"A gripping portrayal of a suburban family in free-fall."
—*Minneapolis Star Tribune*

AN ALGONQUIN READERS ROUND TABLE EDITION WITH READING GROUP GUIDE AND OTHER SPECIAL FEATURES • FICTION • ISBN 978-1-61620-017-6

The Girl Who Fell from the Sky, a novel by Heidi W. Durrow

In the aftermath of a family tragedy, a biracial girl must cope with society's ideas of race and class in this acclaimed novel, winner of the Bellwether Prize for fiction addressing issues of social justice.

Winner of the Bellwether Prize for Fiction

"Affecting, exquisite . . . Durrow's powerful novel is poised to find a place among classic stories of the American experience." — *The Miami Herald*

"Durrow manages that remarkable achievement of telling a subtle, complex story that speaks in equal volumes to children and adults. Like *Catcher in the Rye* or *To Kill a Mockingbird,* Durrow's debut features voices that will ring in the ears long after the book is closed . . . It's a captivating and original tale that shouldn't be missed." — *The Denver Post*

AN ALGONQUIN READERS ROUND TABLE EDITION WITH READING GROUP GUIDE AND OTHER SPECIAL FEATURES • FICTION • ISBN 978-1-61620-015-2

Pictures of You, a novel by Caroline Leavitt

Two women running away from their marriages collide on a foggy highway. The survivor of the fatal accident is left to pick up the pieces not only of her own life but of the lives of the devastated husband and fragile son that the other woman left behind. As these three lives intersect, the book asks, How well do we really know those we love and how do we open our hearts to forgive the unforgivable?

"An expert storyteller . . . Leavitt teases suspense out of the greatest mystery of all—the workings of the human heart." —*Booklist*

"Magically written, heartbreakingly honest . . . Caroline Leavitt is one of those fabulous, incisive writers you read and then ask yourself, Where has she been all my life?"—Jodi Picoult

AN ALGONQUIN READERS ROUND TABLE EDITION WITH READING GROUP GUIDE AND OTHER SPECIAL FEATURES • FICTION • ISBN 978-1-56512-631-2

In the Time of the Butterflies, a novel by Julia Alvarez

In this extraordinary novel, the voices of Las Mariposas (The Butterflies), Minerva, Patria, María Teresa, and Dedé, speak across the decades to tell their stories about life in the Dominican Republic under General Rafael Leonidas Trujillo's dictatorship. Through the art and magic of Julia Alvarez's imagination, the martyred butterflies live again in this novel of valor, love, and the human cost of political oppression.

A National Endowment for the Arts Big Read selection

"A gorgeous and sensitive novel . . . A compelling story of courage, patriotism, and familial devotion." —*People*

"A magnificent treasure for all cultures and all time." —*St. Petersburg Times*

AN ALGONQUIN READERS ROUND TABLE EDITION WITH READING GROUP GUIDE AND OTHER SPECIAL FEATURES • FICTION • ISBN 978-1-56512-976-4

How the García Girls Lost Their Accents, a novel by Julia Alvarez

In Julia Alvarez's brilliant and buoyant first novel, the García sisters, newly arrived from the Dominican Republic, tell their most intimate stories about how they came to be at home—and not at home—in America.

"A clear-eyed look at the insecurity and yearning for a sense of belonging that are part of the immigrant experience . . . Movingly told." —*The Washington Post Book World*

"Subtle . . . Powerful . . . Reveals the intricacies of family, the impact of culture and place, and the profound power of language." —*The San Diego Tribune*

AN ALGONQUIN READERS ROUND TABLE EDITION WITH READING GROUP GUIDE AND OTHER SPECIAL FEATURES • FICTION • ISBN 978-1-56512-975-7

A Reliable Wife, a novel by Robert Goolrick

Rural Wisconsin, 1907. In the bitter cold, Ralph Truitt stands alone on a train platform anxiously awaiting the arrival of the woman who answered his newspaper ad for "a reliable wife." The woman who arrives is not the one he expects in this *New York Times* #1 bestseller about love and madness, longing and murder.

"[A] chillingly engrossing plot . . . Good to the riveting end." —*USA Today*

"Deliciously wicked and tense . . . Intoxicating." —*The Washington Post*

"A rousing historical potboiler." —*The Boston Globe*

AN ALGONQUIN READERS ROUND TABLE EDITION WITH READING GROUP GUIDE AND OTHER SPECIAL FEATURES • FICTION • ISBN 978-1-56512-977-1

Water for Elephants, a novel by Sara Gruen

As a young man, Jacob Jankowski is tossed by fate onto a rickety train, home to the Benzini Brothers Most Spectacular Show on Earth. Amid a world of freaks, grifters, and misfits, Jacob becomes involved with Marlena, the beautiful young equestrian star; her husband, a charismatic but twisted animal trainer; and Rosie, an untrainable elephant who is the great gray hope for this third-rate show. Now in his nineties, Jacob at long last reveals the story of their unlikely yet powerful bonds, ones that nearly shatter them all.

"[An] arresting new novel . . . With a showman's expert timing, [Gruen] saves a terrific revelation for the final pages, transforming a glimpse of Americana into an enchanting escapist fairy tale." —*The New York Times Book Review*

AN ALGONQUIN READERS ROUND TABLE EDITION WITH READING GROUP GUIDE AND OTHER SPECIAL FEATURES • FICTION • ISBN 978-1-56512-560-5

Breakfast with Buddha, a novel by Roland Merullo

When his sister tricks him into taking her guru, a crimson-robed monk, on a trip to their childhood home, Otto Ringling, a confirmed skeptic, is not amused. Six days on the road with an enigmatic holy man who answers every question with a riddle is not what he'd planned. But along the way, Otto is given the remarkable opportunity to see his world—and more important, his life—through someone else's eyes.

"Enlightenment meets *On the Road* in this witty, insightful novel."
—*The Boston Sunday Globe*

"A laugh-out-loud novel that's both comical and wise . . . balancing irreverence with insight." —*The Louisville Courier-Journal*

AN ALGONQUIN READERS ROUND TABLE EDITION WITH READING GROUP GUIDE AND OTHER SPECIAL FEATURES • FICTION • ISBN 978-1-56512-616-9

Between Here and April, a novel by Deborah Copaken Kogan

When a deep-rooted memory suddenly surfaces, Elizabeth Burns becomes obsessed with the long-ago disappearance of her childhood friend April Cassidy.

"The perfect book club book." —*The Washington Post Book World*

"[A] haunting page-turner . . . [A] compelling look at what it means to be a mother and a wife." —*Working Mother*

"Extraordinary . . . This is a story that needs to be told."
—*Elle*, #1 Reader's Pick

AN ALGONQUIN READERS ROUND TABLE EDITION WITH READING GROUP GUIDE AND OTHER SPECIAL FEATURES • FICTION • ISBN 978-1-56512-932-0

Every Last Cuckoo, a novel by Kate Maloy

In the tradition of Jane Smiley and Sue Miller comes this wise and gratifying novel about a woman who gracefully accepts a surprising new role in life just when she thinks her best years are behind her.

Winner of the ALA Reading List Award for Women's Fiction

"Truly engrossing . . . An excellent book club selection." —*Library Journal*

"A tender and wise story of what happens when love lasts."
—Katharine Weber, author of *Triangle*

"Inspiring . . . Grabs the reader by the heart." —*The New Orleans Times-Picayune*

AN ALGONQUIN READERS ROUND TABLE EDITION WITH READING GROUP GUIDE AND OTHER SPECIAL FEATURES • FICTION • ISBN 978-1-56512-675-6

Mudbound, a novel by Hillary Jordan

Mudbound is the saga of the McAllan family, who struggle to survive on a remote ramshackle farm, and the Jacksons, their black sharecroppers. When two men return from World War II to work the land, the unlikely friendship between these brothers-in-arms—one white, one black—arouses the passions of their neighbors. In this award-winning portrait of two families caught up in the blind hatred of a small Southern town, prejudice takes many forms, both subtle and ruthless.

Winner of the Bellwether Prize for Fiction

"This is storytelling at the height of its powers . . . Hillary Jordan writes with the force of a Delta storm." —Barbara Kingsolver

AN ALGONQUIN READERS ROUND TABLE EDITION WITH READING GROUP GUIDE AND OTHER SPECIAL FEATURES • FICTION • ISBN 978-1-56512-677-0

Saving the World, a novel by Julia Alvarez

While Alma Huebner is researching a new novel, she discovers the true story of Isabel Sendales y Gómez, who embarked on a courageous sea voyage to rescue the New World from smallpox. The author of *How the García Girls Lost Their Accents* and *In the Time of the Butterflies* captures the worlds of two women living two centuries apart but with surprisingly parallel fates.

"Fresh and unusual and thought-provokingly sensitive." —*The Boston Globe*

"Engrossing, expertly paced." —*People*

AN ALGONQUIN READERS ROUND TABLE EDITION WITH READING GROUP GUIDE AND OTHER SPECIAL FEATURES • FICTION • ISBN 978-1-56512-558-2